Frederic Lawrence Knowles

Poems of American patriotism, 1776-1898

Frederic Lawrence Knowles

Poems of American patriotism, 1776-1898

ISBN/EAN: 9783337306410

Printed in Europe, USA, Canada, Australia, Japan

Cover: Foto ©Andreas Hilbeck / pixelio.de

More available books at **www.hansebooks.com**

POEMS

OF

AMERICAN PATRIOTISM

1776–1898

SELECTED BY

R. L. PAGET

BOSTON

L. C. PAGE AND COMPANY

(INCORPORATED)

MDCCCXCVIII

DEDICATED TO

George Dewey, U.S.N.

PREFATORY NOTE

SEVERAL collections of patriotic verse have been made, but none hitherto, so far as I know, which carries one later than the Civil War. The present compilation makes pretensions neither to completeness, — a large volume would fail to include everything of merit which has been inspired by national themes, — nor, on the other hand, to a fastidious critical standard. Its only aim is that of presenting anew the noble and popular songs of the past, long endeared to the country's heart, and a still larger amount of stirring contemporary verse, not a little of which has already begun to sing itself into the memory of our time.

Without the kind coöperation of Messrs. Houghton, Mifflin & Company, Messrs. Lee & Shepard, and a few other publishers, it would have been impossible to include several of the finest selections. My thanks are due to them and to all others who have contributed in any way to the success of the book.

CONTENTS.

ix

CONTENTS.

CONTENTS.

xi

CONTENTS.

CONTENTS

To the American Poet.

UNRAVEL all your tangled cheats,
  Your triple-twisted thread conceits, —
Your subtle sonnets fling afar ! —
Stand up and show what man you are !

Why linger o'er decrepit shrine
In Hellas or in Palestine?
America as Greece is grand,
America is Holy Land.

The songs of Nile, and Jordan's tunes
Our sluggish Mississippi croons, —
Lo ! Caught in Erie like a gem
The star that shone o'er Bethlehem !

The age — young, buoyant — longs
    to hear
Its hopes in music high and clear,
Yet ashes o'er your laurels lie,
You rend your garment of the sky.

xv

TO THE AMERICAN POET.

O juggler with the fire divine,
O hoarder of God's bread and wine,
Your dark and doleful sprigs of verse
Nod like the plumes above a hearse.

Behold your birthright !   Cast away
The mess of pottage.   Scorn for aye
The smirking bravo, thin applause, —
Small praise of critics' courts and laws.

Join the great chorus, — all that sings !
Seize the vast harp of divers strings !
What hands have helped that growing
           tone :
Job's, Homer's, Shakespeare's !   Add
           your own !

We want again the note of joy,
The immortal rapture of the boy,
The flame lit quenchless in the dust,
The lips that sing because they must.

A world of wonders wait its song, —
Invention, science, hideous wrong
Heart-smitten by Truth's arrow sharp, —
Up, blinded sceptic !   Grasp your harp !

FREDERIC LAWRENCE KNOWLES.

xvi

POEMS OF PATRIOTISM

POEMS OF
AMERICAN PATRIOTISM.

—·—

America.

MY country, 'tis of thee,
　　Sweet Land of Liberty,
　　Of thee I sing;
Land where my fathers died,
Land of the pilgrims' pride,
From every mountain side
　　Let Freedom ring.

My native country, thee,
Land of the noble free,
　　Thy name I love;
I love thy rocks and rills,
Thy woods and templed hills,
My heart with rapture thrills
　　Like that above.

1

Let music swell the breeze,
And ring from all the trees
    Sweet Freedom's song;
Let mortal tongues awake;
Let all that breathe partake;
Let rocks their silence break,
    The sound prolong.

Our fathers' God, to thee,
Author of Liberty,
    To thee we sing;
Long may our land be bright
With Freedom's holy light;
Protect us by thy might,
    Great God, our King.

Our glorious Land to-day,
'Neath Education's sway,
    Soars upward still.
Its halls of learning fair,
Whose bounties all may share,
Behold them everywhere
    On vale and hill!

Thy safeguard, Liberty,
The school shall ever, be, —
    Our Nation's pride!

AMERICA.

No tyrant hand shall smite,
While with encircling might
All here are taught the Right
    With Truth allied.

Beneath Heaven's gracious will
The star of progress still
    Our course doth sway;
In unity sublime
To broader heights we climb,
Triumphant over Time,
    God speeds our way!

Grand birthright of our sires,
Our altars and our fires
    Keep we still pure!
Our starry flag unfurled,
The hope of all the world,
In Peace and Light impearled,
    God hold secure!
            — *S. F. Smith.*

Columbia, the Gem of the Ocean.

O COLUMBIA, the gem of the ocean,
   The home of the brave and the free,
The shrine of each patriot's devotion,
   A world offers homage to thee!
Thy mandates make heroes assemble,
   When Liberty's form stands in view;
Thy banners make Tyranny tremble,
   When borne by the red, white, and blue.

CHORUS.

When borne by the red, white, and blue,
When borne by the red, white, and blue,
Thy banners make Tyranny tremble,
When borne by the red, white, and blue.

When war winged its wide desolation
   And threatened the land to deform,
The ark then of Freedom's foundation,
   Columbia, rode safe thro' the storm;
With her garlands of vict'ry around her,
   When so proudly she bore her brave
         crew,
With her flag proudly floating before her,
   The boast of the red, white, and blue.

— CHO.

4

The wine-cup, the wine-cup bring hither,
    And fill you it true to the brim;
May the wreaths they have won never
        wither,
    Nor the star of their glory grow dim!
May the service united ne'er sever,
    But they to their colors prove true!
The Army and Navy forever!
    Three cheers for the red, white, and
        blue! — CHO.

Hail, America.

HAIL, son of peak and prairie,
  Triumphant o'er thy foes ! —
Shod with the sands of Cuba,
  Crowned with the Klondike snows !

The breast that nursed thee, shrunk
    with age,
  Still yielded milk of power;
Past kingdoms prophesied thy birth
  And groaned to see thy hour.
Hark ! Egypt moves her lips of stone :
  " For thee I labored long."
Listen !   The isles of Homer :
  " We named thee in our song."

I hear a mighty struggling
  Like grave-clothes torn from death;
Millions of lips unmuffled
  Pour unaccustomed breath :
" Hail, foundling of the western seas,
  Hail, harsh and sacred sod,
Where the strong plant of Freedom
  Holds up its leaves to God !

" For thee our toil, our anguish,
　　The pathos of our years,
Our baths in bleeding battles,
　　Our lives of sweat and tears ! "

　　.　　　.　　　.　　　.　　　.　　　.

Hark ! like a climbing sun, the Voice
　　Mounts upward, — owns the sky,
And clarions from the zenith
　　In trumpet-tongued reply :

" Ye shall no longer wait me,
　　Nor call upon my name,
I come, O buried fathers,
　　The latest fruit of fame !
The Indies pay me tribute,
　　The Andes bring me toll,
I own no serfs but loyal hearts
　　That kiss my kind control.

" My hands are free from slaughter,
　　The sheath conceals the sword,
I trust the regiments of Heaven,
　　And navies of the Lord !
Peace is my guard and angel,
　　Her wings above me stir, —
Mine arms I reach to all the world,
　　Mine eyes I turn to her.

"Yet, ah! if honor's ensign
  Be trampled in the dust,
With angry sorrow let me show
  How strife may still be just;
I will tell History that she lies,
  Even at her very door,
And buy a more enduring peace
  At the red cost of war.

"Trafalgar greets Manila,
  All ages grow divine,
Distance is dead, the Past a dream,
  And Marathon is mine!
Wherever heroes die for truth,
  Beneath whatever sun,
The years are lovers clasping hands,
  And all the world is one!

"O buried sires, your hands are mould —
  That once were hot to slay,
Those eyes are filled with dust, that
      gorged
  With sight of human prey.
Kings tremble on their purple thrones,
  Crowns crumble, tyrants die,
While down untold Millenniums,
  March Destiny and I!"

HAIL, AMERICA.

That tatter'd flag your father kiss'd,
  Fling, boy, against the gale !
And join the cry that rends the sky :
  Hail, home of freedom, hail !
Hail, son of peak and prairie !
  Hail, lord of coast and sea !
Our prayers and song, — our lives
      belong,
  Land of our love, to thee !
          — Frederic Lawrence Knowles.

The Flag.

UP with the banner of the free!
　　Its stars and stripes unfurled!
And let the battle beauty blaze
　　Above a startled world.
No more around its towering staff
　　The folds shall twine again,
Till falls beneath its righteous wrath
　　The gonfalon of Spain.

That flag with constellated stars
　　Shines ever in the van!
And like the rainbow in the storm,
　　Presages peace to man.
For still amid the cannon's roar
　　It sanctifies the fight,
And flames along the battle lines,
　　The emblem of the Right.

It seeks no conquest, knows no fear;
　　Cares not for pomp or state;
As pliant as the atmosphere,
　　As resolute as Fate.

THE FLAG.

Where'er it floats, on land or sea,
  No stain its honor mars,
And Freedom smiles, her fate secure
  Beneath its steadfast stars.

      — Henry Lynden Flash.

Dirge for a Soldier.

CLOSE his eyes; his work is done!
    What to him is friend or foeman,
Rise of moon, or set of sun,
    Hand of man, or kiss of woman?
        Lay him low, lay him low,
        In the clover or the snow!
        What cares he?   He cannot know;
            Lay him low!

As man may, he fought his fight,
    Proved his truth by his endeavor;
Let him sleep in solemn night,
    Sleep forever and forever.
        Lay him low, lay him low,
        In the clover or the snow!
        What cares he?   He cannot know;
            Lay him low!

Fold him in his country's stars,
    Roll the drum and fire the volley!
What to him are all our wars,
    What but death bemocking folly?
        Lay him low, lay him low,
        In the clover or the snow!
        What cares he?   He cannot know;
            Lay him low!

DIRGE FOR A SOLDIER.

Leave him to God's watching eye;
   Trust him to the hand that made him.
Mortal love weeps idly by;
   God alone has power to aid him.
     Lay him low, lay him low,
     In the clover or the snow!
     What cares he? He cannot know!
     Lay him low!
                — G. H. Boker.

Ad Bellonam.

MOTHER of Swords! While the river runs,
  Or the steamer seeks the sea,
While the north wind blows from the chill of Snows,
  And the south from the scented Key,
So long, so long will live the song
  That thy lilting bugles sing,
As the war-ship rides down the deep-sea tides,
Where the green foams white on her armored sides,
  And the wind'ard gun-shields ring.

There be they who sing that the song will cease,
  The song that thy sons began;
That the good old World will loll in peace,
  In the bond of the Peace of Man.
They sing, — and clear 'twixt the notes we hear
  The clink of the warrior's trade;
And the thund'rous call where the hammers fall,
And the steam-power shrieks o'er the factory wall,
  Where the rifled guns are made.

The Breath of the Lord may rule the sea,
  And the Lies of Men the land;
And the craft of the tongue may hold in fee
  The strength of the heavy hand;

But though tongues may quicken and strength may
    sicken,
  And hands grow soft and small,
Year upon year the day draws near
Of the unsheathed sword and the shaken spear,
  That shall make amends for all.

When the Armageddon sunrise breaks
  On the ironclad's smoking line;
When the last dawn lights on that last of fights
  Where the strength of man shall shine,
One last grim day of the world at play
  With bugle and tuck of drum,
While the red drops beat on the shattered fleet,
Till the red sun sinks on the last defeat,
  Then — let the Millennium come!

— Frank L. Pollock.

The Flag That Has Never Known Defeat.

ON history's crimson pages, high up on the roll
of fame.
The story of Old Glory burns, in deathless words of
flame.
'Twas cradled in war's blinding smoke, amid the
roar of guns,
Its lullabies were battle-cries, the shouts of freedom's
sons;
It is the old red, white, and blue, proud emblem of
the free,
It is the flag that floats above our land of liberty.
Then greet it, when you meet it, boys, the flag that
waves on high;
And hats off, all along the line, when freedom's flag
goes by.

CHORUS.

Uncover when the flag goes by, boys,
'Tis freedom's starry banner that you greet,
Flag famed in song and story,
Long may it wave, Old Glory,
The flag that has never known defeat.

All honor to the Stars and Stripes, our glory and
our pride,

All honor to the flag for which our fathers fought
    and died;
On many a blood-stained battle-field, on many a gory
    sea,
The flag has triumphed, evermore triumphant may it
    be.
And since again, 'mid shot and shell, its folds must
    be unfurled,
God grant that we may keep it still unstained before
    the world.
All hail the flag we love, may it victorious ever fly,
And hats off, all along the line, when freedom's flag
    goes by. — CHO.

    — Charles L. Benjamin and George D. Sutton.

The Brave at Home.

THE maid who binds her warrior's sash
　　With smile that well her pain dissembles,
The while beneath her drooping lash
　　One starry tear-drop hangs and trembles,
Though Heaven alone records the tear,
　　And fame shall never know her story,
Her heart has shed a drop as dear
　　As e'er bedewed the field of glory!

The wife who girds her husband's sword
　　'Mid little ones who weep or wonder,
And bravely speaks the cheering word,
　　What though her heart be rent asunder,
Doomed nightly in her dreams to hear
　　The bolts of death around him rattle,
Has shed as sacred blood as e'er
　　Was poured upon the field of battle.

The mother who conceals her grief
　　While to her breast her son she presses,
Then breathes a few brave words and brief,
　　Kissing the patriot brow she blesses,

With no one but her secret God
   To know the pain that weighs upon her,
Sheds holy blood as e'er the sod
   Received on Freedom's field of honor!
                — *Thomas Buchanan Read.*

The Bugle.

IN a glittering glory of diamond dew,
  Where the tall white headstones gleam in a
    row,
By the ivied church, Memorial Day,
  With sheaves of lilies the mourners go.
All but one, and she sits alone,
  A sad-eyed woman with locks of gray,
And keeps a tryst of the vanished years
  With the dear, dead lover who marched away.

Her whitened tresses were brown and bright,
  Her cheeks were pink as a damask rose,
When he clasped her close in a last embrace,
  While about them fluttered the orchard's snows.
The bugle called in the sunlit morn,
  Bayonets glistened, and flags were gay,
He turned to wave her a loud adieu, —
  The brave young lover who marched away.

To the silent city above the town,
  With garlands laden, yet still they pass,
But she seeth only a curly head
  And a broken sword in the trampled grass.

THE BUGLE.

She weaveth a wreath of heliotrope,
  And heareth even the bugle play
That is mute with rust in the mouldered hand
  Of the gallant lover who marched away.

The flowers have fallen about her feet,
  Her lips are pale, and her fingers chill,
Far above the blue of the crystal sky
  Her spirit follows the bugle still.
Its silvery melody leads her on,
  Till far in a world of fadeless May
She plights the troth of her youth again
  With the handsome lover who marched away.

There was never a shot that screamed and fell,
  And never a bayonet-thrust went through
The dauntless breast of a soldier boy,
  But it pierced the heart of a woman, too.
From end to end of the land they sit
  By desolate hearths, alone and gray,
And wait for the ghastly bugle-call
  And the soldier lover who marched away.

              —Minna Irving.

Salute the Flag.

OFF with your hat as the flag goes by!
   And let the heart have its say:
You're man enough for a tear in your eye
   That you will not wipe away.

You're man enough for a thrill that goes
   To your very finger-tips —
Ay! the lump just then in your throat that rose
   Spoke more than your parted lips.

Lift up the boy on your shoulder high,
   And show him the faded shred;
Those stripes would be red as the sunset sky
   If death could have dyed them red.

Off with your hat as the flag goes by!
   Uncover the youngster's head;
Teach him to hold it holy and high
   For the sake of its sacred dead.

                              —*H. C. Bunner.*

War.

I AM War. The upturned eyeballs of piled dead
    men greet my eye,
And the sons of mothers perish, — and I laugh to see
    them die, —
Mine the demon lust for torture, mine the devil lust
    for pain,
And there is to me no beauty like the pale brows of
    the slain !
But my voice calls forth the godlike from the slug-
    gish souls at ease,
And the hands that toyed with ledgers scatter thun-
    ders 'round the seas;
And the lolling idler, wakening, measures up to God's
    own plan,
And the puling trifler greatens to the stature of a
    man.

When I speak, the centuried towers of old cities melt
    in smoke,
And the fortressed ports sink reeling at my far-aimed
    thunder-stroke ;
And an immemorial empire flings its last flag to the
    breeze,
Sinking with its splintered navies down in the unpity-
    ing seas.

But the blind of sight awaken to an unimagined day,
And the mean of soul grow conscious there is great-
    ness in their clay;
Where my bugle voice goes pealing slaves grow
    heroes at its breath,
And the trembling coward rushes to the welcome
    arms of death.

Pagan, heathen and inhuman, devilish as the heart
    of hell,
Wild as chaos, strong for ruin, clothed in hate un-
    speakable, —
So they call me, — and I care not, — still I work my
    waste afar,
Heeding not your weeping mothers and your widows
        — I am War!
But your soft-boned men grow heroes when my flam-
    ing eyes they see,
And I teach your little people how supremely great
    they be;
Yea, I tell them of the wideness of the soul's unfolded
    plan
And the godlike stuff that's moulded in the making of
    a man.

Ah, the godlike stuff that's moulded in the making of
    a man!

WAR.

It has stood my iron testing since this strong old
    world began.
Tell me not that men are weaklings, halting trem-
    blers, pale and slow, —
There is stuff to shame the seraphs in the race of
    men — I know.
I have tested them by fire, and I know that man is
    great,
And the soul of man is stronger than is either death
    or fate ;
And where'er my bugle calls them, under any sun or
    star,
They will leap with smiling faces to the fire test of
    war.

— Sam Walter Foss.

In Action.

WHEN the blue-black waves are tipped with
white, and the balmy trade-winds blow,
When the palm-crowned coast in the offing lies, with
sands like the driven snow,
When the mighty hulls of the battle-ships — the
nation's strength and pride —
And the ghostlike little torpedo-boats are lying side
by side;

When all is still save the screaming gulls, as they
circle high o'erhead,
When naught is heard on the steel-bound decks, save
the watches' measured tread,
When far to windward a tiny cloud floats up from the
grim old fort,
Then the piercing scream of a shrapnel-shot and the
ten-ton gun's report;

Then armored decks are alive with life, and the calls
to quarters below,
Then the gun crews stand beside their guns, and the
stokers sweat below,
Then the jingling bells in the engine-room clamor and
call for speed,

And the thousand tons of hardened steel shake like
    a wind-tossed reed.

Now the guns of the fort are belching flame, and the
    shot and shell fall fast,
Now three are down by the forward gun, and six in
    the fighting mast,
Now the ships rush on in majesty, while the gunners
    hold their breath,
And pray to their God to spare them still from the
    harbor's hidden death.

Now a string of fluttering signal flags from the bridge
    of the flagship fly,
Now the gatlings, rapids, and twelve-inch guns with
    a crashing peal reply,
Now the smoke hangs low o'er the shot-torn wave,
    dark death lurks in the air,
And never a word by the guns is said while they spit
    and boom and flare.

The fleet steams up in battle array, and the broad-
    sides crash and roar,
While the rumble and rip from the enemy's guns
    reply from the smoke-hung shore;
The once white decks run red with blood, while the
    surgeons work below,
And fort and fleet, with shot and shell, pay back each
    blow with blow.

At last a flag of truce is raised and gleams through
    the drifting smoke,
And the havoc and wreck of a gun is seen, where a
    ten-inch shrapnel broke ;
At last the guns of the fleet are still, and now from far
    and near
Are heard the shouts of a victor's crew as they
    answer cheer with cheer.

The shrilly call of the bo's'n's mate the crew from
    quarters pipes,
And the dead are stretched on the quarter-deck,
    wrapped in the stars and stripes,
While the setting sun sinks in the west, a blazing
    ball of fire,
Lighting the scene of a battle fought, and the carnage
    of man's desire.

Somebody's Darling.

INTO a ward of the whitewashed walls,
  Where the dead and the dying lay,
Wounded by bayonet shells and balls,
  Somebody's darling was borne one day, —
Somebody's darling, so young and brave,
  Wearing yet on his sweet, pale face,
Soon to be hid in the dust of the grave,
  The lingering light of his boyhood's grace.

Matted and damp are the curls of gold,
  Kissing the snow of that fair young brow;
Pale are the lips of delicate mould, —
  Somebody's darling is dying now.
Back from his beautiful blue-veined brow
  Brush his wandering waves of gold,
Cross his hands on his bosom now, —
  Somebody's darling is still and cold.

Kiss him once for somebody's sake,
  Murmur a prayer, soft and low;
One bright curl from his fair mates take,
  They were somebody's pride, you know;

29

Somebody's hand hath rested there —
  Was it a mother's, soft and white?
Or have the lips of a sister fair
  Been baptized in those waves of light?

God knows best; he has somebody's love;
  Somebody's heart enshrined him there;
Somebody's wafted his name above
  Night and morn on the wings of prayer;
Somebody wept when he marched away,
  Looking so handsome, brave, and grand;
Somebody's kiss on his forehead lay,
  Somebody clung to his parting hand.

Somebody's watching and waiting for him, —
  Yearning to hold him again to her heart;
And there he lies, with his blue eyes dim,
  And the smiling, childlike lips apart;
Tenderly bury the fair young dead,
  Pausing to drop on his grave a tear;
Carve on the wooden slab at his head:
  "Somebody's Darling slumbers here."

                              — *Maria La Conte.*

The War-ship of 1812.

SHE was no armored cruiser of twice six thousand
tons,
With the thirty foot of metal that make your modern
guns ;
She didn't have a freeboard of thirty-foot in clear,
An' she didn't need a million repairin' fund each
year.
She had no rackin' engines to ramp an' stamp an'
strain,
To work her steel-clad turrets an' break her hull in
twain ;
She did not have electric lights, — the battle-lantern's
glare
Was all the light the 'tween decks had, — an' God's
own good fresh air.

She had no gapin' air-flumes to throw us down our
breath,
An' we didn't batten hatches to smother men to
death ;
She didn't have five hundred smiths — two hundred
men would do —
In the old-time Yankee frigate for an old-time Yankee crew,

An' a fightin' Yankee captain, with his old-time Yankee clothes,
A-cursin' Yankee sailors with his old-time Yankee
oaths.
She was built of Yankee timber and manned by Yankee men,
An' fought by Yankee sailors — Lord send their like
again! .
With the wind abaft the quarter and the sea-foam
flyin' free,
An' every tack and sheet housed taut and braces
eased to lee,
You could hear the deep sea thunder from the knight-
heads where it broke,
As she trailed her lee guns under a blindin' whirl o'
smoke.

She didn't run at twenty knots, — she wasn't built to
run, —
An' we didn't need a half a watch to handle every
gun.
Our captain didn't fight his ship from a little pen o'
steel;
He fought her from his quarter-deck, with two hands
at the wheel,
An' we fought in Yankee fashion, half-naked, —
stripped to board, —

An' when they hauled their red flag down we praised
the Yankee Lord ;
We fought like Yankee sailors, an' we'll do it, too,
again,
You've changed the ships an' methods, but you can't
change Yankee men !

—Philadelphia Record.

The Torpedo-Boat.

SHE'S a floating boiler, crammed with fire and
 steam,
  A toy, with dainty works like any watch;
A working, weaving basketful of tricks, —
  Eccentric, cam and lever, cog and notch.
She's a dashing, lashing, tumbling shell of steel,
  A headstrong, kicking, nervous, plunging beast, —
A long, lean ocean liner, — trimmed down small;
  A bucking bronco harnessed for the east.
    She can rear and toss and roll
    Your body from your soul,
  And she's most unpleasant wet, — to say the least!

But see her slip in; sneaking down, at night,
  All a-tremble, deadly, silent, — Satan-sly.
Watch her gather for the rush, and catch her breath!
  See her dodge the wakeful cruiser's sweeping eye.
Hear the humming! Hear her coming! coming fast!
  (That's the sound might make men wish they were
    at home
— Hear the rattling Maxim, barking rapid fire!)
  See her loom out through the fog with bows
    afoam!

34

THE TORPEDO-BOAT.

Then some will wish for land.
(They 'd be sand fleas in the sand;
Or yellow grubs reposing in the loam !)

She's a floating boiler, crammed with fire and steam,
   A dainty toy, with works just like a watch;
A weaving, working basketful of tricks, —
   A pent volcano, and stoppered at top-notch.
She is Death and swift Destruction in a case
   (Not the Unseen, but the Awful, — plain in sight),
The Dread that must be halted when afar;
   She's a concentrated, fragile form of Might !
      She's a daring, vicious thing,
      With a rending, deadly sting, —
And she asks no odds nor quarter in the fight !

                              —*James Barnes.*

Old Flag Forever.

SHE'S up there, — Old Glory, — where lightnings
    are sped;
She dazzles the nations with ripples of red;
And she'll wave for us living, or droop o'er us
    dead, —
The flag of our country forever!
She's up there, — Old Glory, — how bright the stars
    stream!
And the stripes like red signals of liberty gleam!
And we dare for her, living, or dream the last dream,
'Neath the flag of our country forever!
She's up there, — Old Glory, — no tyrant-dealt scars,
No blur on her brightness, no stain on her stars!
The brave blood of heroes hath crimsoned her bars.
She's the flag of our country forever!

                    —Frank L. Stanton.

The Flag.

ROLL a river wide and strong,
  Like the tides a-swinging.
Lift the joyful floods of song,
  Set the mountains ringing.
Run the lovely banner high, —
  Crimson morning-glory!
Field as blue as yonder sky,
  Every star a story.

Let the people, heart and lip,
  Hail the gleaming splendor!
Let the guns from shore and ship
  Acclamation render!
All ye oceans, clap your hands!
  Echo plains and highlands,
Speed the voice thro' all the lands
  To the Orient islands.

Darling flag of liberty!
  Law and Love revealing,
All the downcast turn to thee,
  For thy help appealing.
In the front for human right,
  Flash thy stars of morning,

All that hates and hides the light
  Flies before thy warning.

By the colors of the day,
  By the breasts that wear them,
To the living God we pray
  For the brave that bear them !
Run the rippling banner high ;
  Peace or war the weather,
Cheers or tears, we'll live or die
  Under it together.

                           — *M. W. S.*

Columbia.

MATED to the Millennium, — Time's last heir
  And proudest daughter, conquerless as he;
Girdled with lakes like jewels princely fair,
  With strong feet planted in the Mexic sea!

Where Law is liberty, where Love is power,
  And the twain one, there Treason cannot dwell;
A fangless asp, it coiled one impotent hour,
  But at thy white glance backward writhed to hell.

Leave dotard empires flames of drunken war,
  Be thine chaste hours of labor and increase,
Vineyards and harvests yielding guiltless store,
  Toil's bloodless battles on the plains of peace!

Yet when slain Weakness, dying at thy door,
  Summoning thy right arm's vengeance, clasps thy
    feet, —
Thy sword that drinks her murderer's blood is pure
  As laughing sickles in the saffron wheat.

39

Clearing a crimson path where Peace may tread
  More safely; thou dost play thy patient part,
Love's pledged ally, — yea, though thy blade be red;
  Thrusting War's weapons thro' his own false heart.

O goddess, arctic-crowned and tropic-shod
  And belted with great waters, hear our cry, —
More honest never reached the ear of God, —
  We'll serve thee, laud thee, love thee, till we die!

                — *Frederic Lawrence Knowles.*

Song of the Bullet.

I T whizzed and whistled along the blurred
　　And red-blent ranks ; and it nicked the star
Of an epaulette, as it snarled the word, —
　　　　War !

On he sped, — and the lifted wrist
　　Of the ensign-bearer stung, and straight
Dropped at his side, as the word was hissed, —
　　　　Hate !

On went the missile, — smoothed the blue
　　Of a jaunty cap, and the curls thereof,
Cooing soft, as a dove might do, —
　　　　Love !

Sang ! — sang on ! — sang hate, — sang war, —
　　Sang love, in sooth, till it needs must cease,
Hushed in the heart it was questing, or, —
　　　　Peace !

　　　　　　—James Whitcomb Riley.

The Song of the Cannon.

WHEN the diplomats cease from their
    capers,
  Their red-tape requests and replies,
Their shuttlecock battle of papers,
  Their saccharine parley of lies;
When the plenipotentiary wrangle
  Is tied in a chaos of knots,
And becomes an unwindable tangle
  Of verbals unmarried to thoughts;
When they've anguished and argued pro-
    foundly,
  Asserted, assumed, and averred,
Then I end up the dialogue roundly
  With my monosyllabical word.

Not mine is a speech academic,
  No lexicon lingo is mine,
And in politic parley, polemic,
  I was never created to shine.
But I speak with some show of decision,
  And I never attempt to be bland,
I hurl my one word with precision,
  My hearers — they all understand.

THE SONG OF THE CANNON.

It requires no labored translation,
   Its pith and its import to glean;
They gather its signification,
   They know at the first what I mean.

The codes of the learned legations,
   Of form, and of rule, and decree,
The etiquette books of the nations, —
   They were never intended for me.
When your case is talked into confusion,
   Then hush you, my diplomat friend,
Give me just a word in conclusion,
   Let me bring the dispute to an end.
Ye diplomats, cease to aspire
   A case that's appealed to debate,
It has gone to a court that is higher,
   And I'm the Attorney for Fate.
                    — *Sam Walter Foss.*

The Volunteer.

" AT dawn," he said, " I bid them all farewell,
To go where bugles call and rifles gleam."
And with the restless thought asleep he fell,
And glided into dream.

A great hot plain from sea to mountain spread, —
Through it a level river slowly drawn;
He moved with a vast crowd, and at its head
Streamed banners like the dawn.

There came a blinding flash, a deafening roar,
And dissonant cries of triumph and dismay;
Blood trickled down the river's reedy shore,
And with the dead he lay.

The morn broke in upon his solemn dreams,
And still with steady pulse and deepening eye,
" Where bugles call," he said, " and rifles gleam,
I follow, though I die!"

Wise youth! By few is glory's wreath attained;
But death, or late or soon, awaiteth all,
To fight in Freedom's cause is something gained, —
And nothing lost to fall.

— *Elbridge Jefferson Cutler.*

The Flag Goes By.

HATS off!
Along the street there comes
A blare of bugles, a ruffle of drums,
A flash of color beneath the sky.
Hats off!
The flag is passing by!

Blue, and crimson, and white it shines,
Over the steel-tipped, ordered lines.
Hats off!
The colors before us fly;
But more than the flag is passing by.

Sea fights and land fights, grim and great,
Fought to make and to save the state;
Weary marches and sinking ships;
Cheers of victory on dying lips;

Days of plenty, and years of peace,
March of a strong land's swift increase;
Equal justice, right, and law,
Stately honor and reverend awe;

Sign of a Nation, great and strong,
To ward her people from foreign wrong;

45

Pride, and glory, and honor, all
Live in the colors to stand or fall.

Hats off!
Along the street there comes
A blare of bugles, a ruffle of drums;
And loyal hearts are beating high.
Hats off!
The flag is passing by!

Song of the Battle-ships.

MIND of man, what have you wrought,
  From the ribs of mother earth,
From the soil that gave you birth?
Mind of man, what have you wrought?

You have builded mighty navies, you have made the
    sea your slave,
And the booming of your cannon strikes the crest of
    every wave;

You have dug into the bowels of the earth's eternal
    hills,
Tearing out the stubborn metals for the grinding of
    your mills;

For the forging of your hammers, for the blowing of
    your blasts,
For the making of your armor, for the building of
    your masts;

For the guns whose rolling thunders frighten half a
    world in awe,
Shouting out the fateful message, " Right is Might,
    and Might is Law."

Oh, the guns, great guns,
Shooting forty million tons;
Shooting death, and shooting hell!
Aim, you gunners, aim them well.

You have slaved a million freemen for the digging of
your coal,
For your engines throbbing wildly, like a panting
human soul.

You have chained the ragged lightning, and you hold
it in your hand,
By the pressing of a button you can devastate a land.

Oh, the fury of your anger! Oh, the pent-up seas
of blood
That shall wet the ocean's battles with a gory, human flood!

Oh, the booming of your cannon! Oh, the millions
you shall slay,
When the wrath of man is loosened in a frightful
judgment day!

Mind of man, what have you wrought,
From the ribs of mother earth,
From the soil that gave you birth?
Mind of man, what have you wrought?
— *C. F. Harper.*

The Soldier Boy for Me.

THE man who wears the shoulder-straps
And has his sword in hand,
Who proudly strides along in front,
Looks good, and brave, and grand;
But, back there in the ranks somewhere, —
Just which I cannot see, —
With his gun upon his shoulder, is
The soldier boy for me!

The man who wears the shoulder-straps
Is handsome, brave, and true,
But there are other handsome boys,
And other brave ones, too!
When there are heights that must be won
While bullets fill the air,
'Tis not the officer alone
Who braves the dangers there.

The man who wears the shoulder-straps
Is cheered along the way,
And public honor dulls his dread
Of falling in the fray;
But, there behind him in the ranks,
And moving like a part

Of some machine, is many a man
   With just as brave a heart.

The man who wears the shoulder-straps
   Deserves the people's praise;
I honor and applaud him for
   The noble part he plays;
But, back there in the ranks somewhere,
   Stout-hearted, brave, is he, —
Prepared to do, and nerved to dare, —
   The soldier boy for me!

                        —S. E. Kiser.

The Harbor Mine.

GIVE the speedway to the cruiser,
  Give the monitor the tide,
To the battle-ship with its steel side-strip
  The channel deep and wide;
Give the fleet full way o'er the ocean,
  Give the batt'ries wind-wide range;
But mine be a grave 'neath the salt-sea wave,
  'Mid the creatures wild and strange,
      For I am the harbor mine,
        And day by day I swing
      On my anchor-chain 'neath the rolling
        main
        While the billows sadly sing.
      Yea, I am the harbor mine.
        And I am the monster fell
      For those who tread upon my head
        As they would on a hidden hell.

Give the broad sea course to the steel-girt horse
  That champs on the rolling foam,
And give the breadth of the leagueless tide
  To the fleets that coastwise roam;
But give me a rest 'neath the billows' crest,
  As, oh, they sweetly sing

Of the world above where they dream of love
　And the earth grows bright with spring.
　　For I am the harbor mine.
　　　They whisper : " Don't go there,
　　He's the avatar of the woe of man,
　　　Of sorrow and despair."
　　They know not where I hide,
　　　And they dare not track my den,
　　For I am the flame of the under-deep
　　　And I feed on mangled men.

Give the wind to the merchant-liners,
　The channel to the fleet;
In the harbor mouth, by North by South,
　For the coming of their feet
I wait through the weary hours,
　And they search for me in vain,
For I am the hidden hell that sleeps
　In the crib of the under-main.
　　Oh, I am the harbor mine !
　　　The sea-gulls come and go,
　　Above the sun and the stars that shine
　　　Smile on me here below;
　　But the ship that sails my way,
　　　Ah, who shall count the wrack
　　Of the shriven plates as the lightning leaps
　　　Along the magnet's track !

THE HARBOR MINE.

For a keen eye in the portals,
  With a hand upon the key,
From the fortress waits to tell the fates
  Of the ships that sail to me.
The battle-ship or cruiser,
  The children of the fleet, —
To all that come with a welcome glum
  I'm here to trip their feet.
     Yea, I am the harbor mine,
       With the lightning in my hand,
     And I guard the ports, and hold the forts,
       When the ships above me land.
     I rock on the under-ocean,
       In the gloom of my deep salt-den.
     And I am the hell that hidden waits
       To feed on the shapes of men.

To feed on the guns that thundered,
  To feed on the plates and bars,
When the ship sinks down in the channel
  To me and the ghosts and stars ;
·To feed on the smashed projectiles,
  To feed on the grim barbette, —
All day I wait in the harbor's gate,
  All day my anchors fret.
     For I am the harbor mine,
       Whose voice is a muffled roar,

Whose song is a flash of the magnet's fire
  In the opera of war.
And they whisper: " Don't go there,
  For he is a monster fell,
And ships must tread upon his head
  As they would on a hidden hell."

                — F. McK.

A Soldier's Heart.

WHERE is the heart of a soldier,
  His thought, his hope, and his dream,
When the rifles ring and the bullets sing,
  And the flashing sabres gleam?
Oh, not on the field of battle,
  But far and far away,
His heart is living the old, old hopes,
  While his sword is red in the fray!

Where is the heart of a soldier,
  And what do the bugles wake,
And what does the roar of the cannon mean
  When the hills beneath them shake?
Oh, not for him the glory,
  And the dash and the crash of war,
But his heart is away on a mission gay
  Where they hear no cannon roar!

And there is the heart of a soldier, —
  A little home on the hill,
A white-faced woman, a little child,
  That stands by the window-sill;
A little song, and a little prayer,
  And a wonder in the face,

And a " God save papa, and bring him back
  In the goodness of thy grace ! "

And there is the heart of a soldier, —
  Not on the field of fight,
But steeped in the dream of a saddened home
  Where a window keeps its light,
That a soldier's feet may keep the path,
  And his way may homeward lead,
When under the flag of the freedom-land
  He has wrought the hero's deed.

Yea, there is the heart of a soldier,
  Where wife and baby are ;
Though his eyes and his will may follow
  The light of the battle star ;
Though his hand may swing the sabre,
  And his bayonet charge the foe,
The soldier's heart is away, away,
  In the home where they miss him so !

                             —Baltimore News.

The Song of Then and Now.

OH, they sang a song of Wind and Sail
   In the days of heave and haul,
Of the weather-gage, of tack and sheet,
When the anchor rose to the tramp of feet,
And the click of the capstan pawl.
They sang brave songs of the old broadsides,
   Long Tom, and the carronade!
Hi! cutlass and pike, as the great sides strike, —
   Ho! the cheers of the ne'er-afraid!
For they cheered as they fought, did those sailor-
      men;
   They stripped to the buff for the fray, —
It was steel to steel, it was eye to eye, —
Yard-arm to yard-arm against the sky!
   All ye boarders, up and away!

  .   .   .   .

They sang of the men on the quarter-deck, —
   Brave deeds of those captains bold!
Never a name but was known to fame,
   And was praised in the days of old.
Let us sing the song of the fighting men,
   The sail and the plunging bow, —
The good old song of the Sea and the Ship,
   The song of the Then and Now!

Gone are the days of the heave and haul
  (Think ye our blood has thinned?);
We're slaves of steam and science,
  Not toilers of the wind!
Oh, the cable comes in to the cable tiers,
  And no one lifts a hand;
The click of a bell sounds out, " That's well ! "
  And the engines understand!
We come in 'gainst the wind and the tide at
      night,
  And go out 'gainst the storm in the morn.
(But think ye our arms have lost their might?
  Think ye our locks are shorn?)

Past are the days of Wind and Sail,
  We've cast off the thrall of the sea,
We take no heed of the weather-gage, —
  No fear of the rocks on the lee.
We can come and go in the fiercest blow
  (It is food for our roaring fires!),
For the great screw churns, and the huge hull
      turns
  As the Soul of the Ship desires!
But the spirit, the strength, and the will are there,
  The sea has not changed her men;
The ship must do, and the men must dare,
  And Now is the same as Then!

THE SONG OF THEN AND NOW.

They raked and they fought at pistol-shot, —
  We fight at two miles and more.
(Think ye their dangers discount ours,
  Ye men of books ashore?)
The turret turns and the guns are trained, —
  But not in the older way;
The conning-tower is the one-man power
  And the Soul of the Ship holds sway.
But in sponson, turret, and great barbette,
  Or below in the noxious air,
Are brave forms covered with blood and sweat, —
  The fighting men are there!

There are dangers our father wot not of
  (In the days of wind and sail):
The unseen foes and the sighted Death,
  With the foam along the rail.
The channels are filled with uncouth shapes
  That lurk below in the brine, —
The force of fifty ships is there
  In the sullen, sunken mine!
Tho' no orders come from the quarter-deck,
  Hear the rip of the rapid fire!
Full speed ahead, astern, or check,
  At a spark from the semaphore wire!

And the ship she trembles from top to keel, —
  Tho' she rates twelve thousand tons!

And her scorched decks leap with a thundering
    throb
  'Neath the roar of her twelve-inch guns!
Dented, and tortured, and pierced, she stands
  The blows on her ringing plates;
Grimy and blank she signals back
  To the flags of her fighting mates.
Hear the grinding crash from her armored prow,
  Hear the rattling Colts from the mast?
Young " Steel Flanks " of the living Now
  Is " Old Ironsides " of the past!

Oh, then here's to the men, where'er they be, —
  The men of steel and steam!
They're the same old stock from the parent
    block, —
  When they welcomed the wind abeam.
Tho' one shot may equal a broadside's weight,
  One blow may decide the fight,
They serve their guns, they aim them straight,
  And the Flag will be kept in sight!
The old captains bold, — cocked hats and gold, —
  Were made for their country's hour,
And the Soul of the Ship proclaims the mould
  Of the mind in the conning-tower!

.   .   .   .

THE SONG OF THEN AND NOW.

Let us sing the song of Wind and Sail, —
　　Brave deeds of the captains bold !
Never a name but was known to fame,
　　And was praised in the days of old.
Let us sing the song of the armored ship,
　　With the ramming, roaring bow !
For the Flag is the same, the men are the same, —
　　'Tis the song of Then and Now !

　　　　　　　　　　—*James Barnes.*

THE REVOLUTIONARY WAR

Warren's Address.

STAND! the ground's your own, my
       braves!
Will ye give it up to slaves?
Will ye look for greener graves?
       Hope ye mercy still?
What's the mercy despots feel?
Hear it in that battle peal!
Read it on yon bristling steel!
       Ask it, — ye who will.

Fear ye foes who kill for hire?
Will ye to your homes retire?
Look behind you! — they're afire!
       And, before you, see
Who have done it!   From the vale
On they come! — and will ye quail?
Leaden rain and iron hail
       Let their welcome be!

In the God of battles trust!
Die we may, — and die we must;
But, oh, where can dust to dust
       Be consign'd so well,

65

As where Heaven its dews shall shed
On the martyr'd patriot's bed,
And the rocks shall raise their head
   Of his deeds to tell?

— John Pierpont.

Nathan Hale.

TO drum-beat and heart-beat,
  A soldier marches by;
There is color in his cheek,
  There is courage in his eye,
Yet to drum-beat and heart-beat
  In a moment he must die.

By starlight and moonlight,
  He seeks the Briton's camp;
He hears the rustling flag,
  And the armèd sentry's tramp;
And the starlight and moonlight
  His silent wanderings lamp.

With slow tread and still tread,
  He scans the tented line;
And he counts the battery guns,
  By the gaunt and shadowy pine;
And his slow tread and still tread
  Gives no warning sign.

The dark wave, the plumed wave,
  It meets his eager glance;
And it sparkles 'neath the stars,
  Like the glimmer of a lance, —

A dark wave, a plumed wave,
　On an emerald expanse.

A sharp clang, a still clang,
　And terror in the sound!
For the sentry, falcon-eyed,
　In the camp a spy hath found;
With a sharp clang, a steel clang,
　The patriot is bound.

With calm brow, and steady brow,
　He listens to his doom;
In his look there is no fear,
　Nor a shadow-trace of gloom;
But with calm brow and steady brow
　He robes him for the tomb.

In the long night, the still night,
　He kneels upon the sod;
And the brutal guards withhold
　E'en the solemn word of God!
In the long night, the still night,
　He walks where Christ hath trod.

'Neath the blue morn, the sunny morn,
　He dies upon the tree;
And he mourns that he can lose
　But one life for Liberty;

NATHAN HALE.

And in the blue morn, the sunny morn,
   His spent wings are free.

But his last words, his message-words,
   They burn, lest friendly eye
Should read how proud and calm
   A patriot could die,
With his last words, his dying words,
   A soldier's battle-cry.

From Fame-leaf and Angel-leaf,
   From monument and urn,
The sad of earth, the glad of heaven,
   His tragic fate shall learn;
And on Fame-leaf and Angel-leaf
   The name of HALE shall burn!

                — *Francis M. Finch.*

The Old Continentals.

IN their ragged regimentals
　　Stood the old Continentals,
　　　　Yielding not,
When the grenadiers were lunging,
And like hail fell the plunging
　　　　Cannon-shot ;
　　　　When the files
　　　　Of the isles
From the smoky night-encampment bore the banner
　　of the rampant
　　　　Unicorn,
And grummer, grummer, grummer rolled the roll of
　　the drummer,
　　　　Through the morn !

　　Then with eyes to the front all,
　　And with guns horizontal
　　　　Stood our sires ;
　　And the balls whistled deadly,
　　And in streams flashing redly
　　　　Blazed the fires ;
　　　　As the roar
　　　　On the shore,

THE OLD CONTINENTALS.

Swept the strong battle breakers o'er the green
    sodded acres
        Of the plain ;
And louder, louder, louder cracked the black gun-
    powder,
        Cracking amain !

      Now like smiths at their forges
      Worked the red Saint George's
         Cannoneers ;
      And the " villainous saltpetre "
      Rung a fierce, discordant metre
         Round their ears;
         As the swift
         Storm drift,
With hot, sweeping anger, came the horse-guard's
    clangor
        On our flanks,
Then higher, higher, higher burned the old-fashioned
    fire
        Through the ranks !

      Then the old-fashioned colonel
      Galloped through the white, infernal
         Powder cloud ;
      And his broad sword was swinging,

And his brazen throat was ringing
Trumpet loud.
Then the blue
Bullets flew,
And the trooper jackets redden at the touch of the
leaden
Rifle breath ;
And rounder, rounder, rounder roared the iron six-
pounder
Hurling death !
— *Guy Humphrey McMaster.*

Columßia.

Written during the author's service as an army chaplain, 1777-78.

COLUMBIA, Columbia, to glory arise,
   The queen of the world, and the child of
      the skies;
Thy genius commands thee; with rapture
      behold,
While ages on ages thy splendor unfold!
Thy reign is the last, and the noblest of time,
Most fruitful thy soil, most inviting thy clime;
Let the crimes of the east ne'er encrimson thy
      name,
Be freedom, and science, and virtue thy fame.

To conquest and slaughter let Europe aspire;
Whelm nations in blood, and wrap cities in fire;
Thy heroes the rights of mankind shall defend,
And triumph pursue them, and glory attend;
A world is thy realm: for a world be thy laws,
Enlarged as thine empire, and just as thy cause;
On Freedom's broad basis, that empire shall rise,
Extend with the main, and dissolve with the
      skies.

Fair science her gates to thy sons shall unbar,
And the east see the morn hide the beams of
      her star.
New bards, and new sages, unrivalled shall soar
To fame unextinguished, when time is no more;
To thee, the last refuge of virtue designed,
Shall fly from all nations the best of mankind;
Here, grateful to heaven, with transport shall
      bring
Their incense, more fragrant than odors of spring.

Nor less shall thy fair ones to glory ascend,
And genius and beauty in harmony blend;
The graces of form shall awake pure desire,
And the charms of the soul ever cherish the fire;
Their sweetness unmingled, their manners
      refined,
And virtue's bright image, instamped on the mind,
With peace and soft rapture shall teach life to
      glow,
And light up a smile in the aspect of woe.

Thy fleets to all regions thy power shall display,
The nations admire and the ocean obey;
Each shore to thy glory its tribute unfold,
And the east and the south yield their spices
      and gold.

As the day-spring unbounded, thy splendor shall
    flow,
And earth's little kingdoms before thee shall bow;
While the ensigns of union, in triumph unfurled,
Hush the tumult of war and give peace to the
    world.

Thus, as down a lone valley, with cedars o'er-
    spread,
From war's dread confusion I pensively strayed,
The gloom from the face of fair heaven retired;
The winds ceased to murmur; the thunders
    expired;
Perfumes as of Eden flowed sweetly along,
And a voice as of angels enchantingly sung:
"Columbia, Columbia, to glory arise,
The queen of the world, and the child of the
    skies."
                    — *Timothy Dwight.*

Song of Marion's Men.

OUR band is few, but true and tried,
　　Our leader frank and bold;
The British soldier trembles
　　When Marion's name is told.
Our fortress is the good greenwood,
　　Our tent the cypress-tree;
We know the forest round us,
　　As seamen know the sea;
We know its walls of thorny vines,
　　Its glades of reedy grass,
Its safe and silent islands
　　　Within the dark morass.

Woe to the English soldiery
　　That little dread us near!
On them shall light at midnight
　　A strange and sudden fear;
When, waking to their tents on fire,
　　They grasp their arms in vain,
And they who stand to face us
　　Are beat to earth again;
And they who fly in terror deem
　　A mighty host behind,

And hear the tramp of thousands
  Upon the hollow wind.

Then sweet the hour that brings release
  From danger and from toil;
We talk the battle over,
  And share the battle's spoil.
The woodland rings with laugh and
      shout,
  As if a hunt were up,
And woodland flowers are gathered
  To crown the soldier's cup.
With merry songs we mock the wind
  That in the pine-top grieves,
And slumber long and sweetly
  On beds of oaken leaves.

Well knows the fair and friendly moon
  The band that Marion leads, —
The glitter of their rifles,
  The scampering of their steeds.
'Tis life to guide the fiery barb
  Across the moonlight plain;
'Tis life to feel the night wind
  That lifts his tossing mane.
A moment in the British camp, —
  A moment, — and away

Back to the pathless forest,
  Before the peep of day.

Grave men there are by broad Santee,
  Grave men with hoary hairs;
Their hearts are all with Marion,
  For Marion are their prayers.
And lovely ladies greet our band
  With kindliest welcoming,
With smiles like those of summer,
  And tears like those of spring.
For them we wear these trusty arms,
  And lay them down no more
Till we have driven the Briton
  Forever from our shore.

— *William Cullen Bryant.*

Hail, Columbia.

HAIL, Columbia! happy land!
  Hail, ye heroes! heaven-born band!
Who fought and bled in Freedom's cause,
Who fought and bled in Freedom's cause,
And when the storm of war was gone,
Enjoyed the peace your valor won;
Let independence be your boast,
Ever mindful what it cost,
Ever grateful for the prize,
Let its altar reach the skies.

CHORUS.

  Firm united let us be,
  Rallying round our liberty,
  As a band of brothers joined,
  Peace and safety we shall find.

Immortal patriots, rise once more,
Defend your rights, defend your shore;
Let no rude foe with impious hand,
Let no rude foe with impious hand
Invade the shrine where sacred lies
Of toil and blood the well-earned prize;

79

While offering peace, sincere and just,
In Heaven we place a manly trust
That truth and justice may prevail,
And every scheme of bondage fail. — CHO.

Sound, sound the trump of fame!
Let Washington's great name
Ring thro' the world with loud applause!
Ring thro' the world with loud applause!
Let every clime to freedom dear
Listen with a joyful ear;
With equal skill, with steady pow'r,
He governs in the fearful hour
Of horrid war, or guides with ease
The happier time of honest peace. — CHO.

Behold the chief who now commands,
Once more to serve his country stands!
The rock on which the storm was beat!
The rock on which the storm was beat!
But armed in virtue, firm and true,
His hopes are fixed on heaven and you.
When hope was sinking in dismay,
When gloom obscured Columbia's day,
His steady mind, from changes free,
Resolved on death or liberty. — CHO.

—Joseph Hopkinson.

WAR OF 1812

Old Ironsides.

AY, tear her tattered ensign down,
　　Long has it waved on high,
And many an eye has danced to see
　　That banner in the sky;
Beneath it rung the battle-shout,
　　And burst the cannon's roar;
The meteor of the ocean air
　　Shall sweep the clouds no more!

Her deck, once red with heroes' blood,
　　Where knelt the vanquished foe,
When winds were hurrying o'er the flood,
　　And waves were white below,
No more shall feel the victor's tread,
　　Or know the conquered knee;
The harpies of the shore shall pluck
　　The eagle of the sea!

Oh, better that her shattered hulk
　　Should sink beneath the wave!
Her thunders shook the mighty deep,
　　And there should be her grave:

83

Nail to the mast her holy flag,
Set every threadbare sail;
And give her to the god of storms,
The lightning and the gale!

— *Oliver Wendell Holmes.*

𝕿𝖍𝖊 𝕾𝖙𝖆𝖗 𝕾𝖕𝖆𝖓𝖌𝖑𝖊𝖉 𝕭𝖆𝖓𝖓𝖊𝖗.

OH, say, can you see, by the dawn's early light,
  What so proudly we hailed at the twilight's
    last gleaming?
Whose broad stripes and bright stars thro' the peril-
    ous fight
  O'er the ramparts we watched were so gallantly
    streaming?
And the rockets' red glare and bombs bursting in air
  Gave proof thro' the night that our flag was still
    there;
Oh, say, does that Star Spangled Banner yet wave
  O'er the land of the free and the home of the
    brave?

CHORUS.

Oh, say, does the Star Spangled Banner yet wave
O'er the land of the free and the home of the brave?

On the shore, dimly seen thro' the mist of the deep,
  Where the foe's haughty host in dread silence
    reposes,
What is that which the breeze o'er the towering
    steep,
  As it fitfully blows, half conceals, half discloses?

Now it catches the gleam of the morning's first beam,
In full glory reflected now shines in the stream;
'Tis the Star Spangled Banner, oh, long may it
wave
O'er the land of the free and the home of the
brave. — Cho.

And where is that band who so vauntingly swore,
'Mid the havoc of war and the battle's confusion,
A home and a country they'd leave us no more?
Their blood has washed out their foul footsteps'
pollution.
No refuge could save the hireling and slave
From terror of flight or the gloom of the grave;
And the Star Spangled Banner in triumph doth
wave
O'er the land of the free and the home of the
brave. — Cho.

Oh, thus be it ever, when freemen shall stand
Between their loved home and the war's desolation;
Blest with victory and peace, may the Heaven-res-
cued land
Praise the Power that made and preserved us a
nation!

THE STAR SPANGLED BANNER.

Then conquer we must, when our cause it is just,
   And this be our motto, " In God is our trust ! "
And the Star Spangled Banner in triumph shall wave
   O'er the land of the free and the home of the
      brave. — CHO.

                                    — *Francis Scott Key*.

Yankee Thunders.

BRITANNIA'S gallant streamers
  Float proudly o'er the tide,
And fairly wave Columbia's stripes,
  In battle side by side.
And ne'er did bolder seamen meet,
  Where ocean's surges pour;
O'er the tide now they ride,
  While the bell'wing thunders roar,
While the cannon's fire is flashing fast,
  And the bell'wing thunders roar.

When Yankee meets the Briton,
  Whose blood congenial flows,
By Heav'n created to be friends,
  By fortune rendered foes;
Hard then must be the battle fray,
  Ere well the fight is o'er;
Now they ride, side by side,
  While the bell'wing thunders roar,
While her cannon's fire is flashing fast,
  And the bell'wing thunders roar.

Still, still, for noble England
  Bold D'Acres's streamers fly;

YANKEE THUNDERS.

And for Columbia, gallant Hull's
   As proudly and as high;
Now louder rings the battle din,
   And thick the volumes pour;
Still they ride, side by side,
   While the bell'wing thunders roar,
While the cannon's fire is flashing fast,
   And the bell'wing thunders roar.

Why lulls Britannia's thunder,
   That waked the wat'ry war?
Why stays the gallant *Guerrière*,
   Whose streamers waved so fair?
That streamer drinks the ocean's wave,
   That warrior's fight is o'er!
Still they ride, side by side,
   While the bell'wing thunders roar,
While the cannon's fire is flashing fast,
   And the bell'wing thunders roar.

Hark! 'tis the Briton's lee gun!
   Ne'er bolder warrior kneeled!
And ne'er to gallant mariners
   Did braver seamen yield.
Proud be the sires, whose hardy boys
   Then fell to fight no more;

With the brave, 'mid the wave,
　When the cannon's thunders roar,
Their spirits then shall trim the blast,
　And swell the thunder's roar.

Vain were the cheers of Britons,
　Their hearts did vainly swell,
Where virtue, skill, and bravery
　With gallant Morris fell.
That heart so well in battle tried,
　Along the Moorish shore,
And again o'er the main,
　When Columbia's thunders roar,
Shall prove its Yankee spirit true,
　When Columbia's thunders roar.

Hence be our floating bulwark
　Those oaks our mountains yield;
'Tis mighty Heaven's plain decree, —
　Then take the wat'ry field!
To ocean's farthest barrier then
　Your whit'ning sail shall pour;
Safe they'll ride o'er the tide,
　While Columbia's thunders roar,
While her cannon's fire is flashing fast,
　And her Yankee thunders roar.

1813.

Our Navy.

ON wings of glory, swift as light,
  The sound of battle came,
The gallant Hull in glorious fight
  Has won the wreaths of fame.

CHORUS.

Let brave Columbia's noble band
  With hearts united rise,
Swear to protect their native land
  Till sacred freedom dies.

Let brave Decatur's dauntless breast
  With patriot ardor glow,
And in the garb of vict'ry drest
  Triumphant blast the foe. — CHO.

And Rogers with his gallant crew
  O'er the wide ocean ride,
To prove their loyal spirits true,
  And crush old Albion's pride. — CHO.

Then hail another *Guerrière* there,
  With roaring broadsides hail;
And while the thunder rends the air
  See Briton's sons turn pale. — CHO.

"The day is ours, my boys, huzza!"
  The great commander cries,
While all responsive roar huzza!
  With pleasure-sparkling eyes. — Cho.

Thus shall Columbia's fame be spread,
  Her heaven-born eagle soar;
Her deeds of glory shall be read
  When tyrants are no more. — Cho.

1813.

The Constitution's Last Fight.

A YANKEE ship and a Yankee crew —
    Constitution, where ye bound for?
Wherever, my lad, there's fight to be had
    Acrost the Western ocean.

Our captain was married in Boston town
    And sailed next day to sea;
For all must go when the State says so;
    Blow high, blow low, sailed we.

" Now, what shall I bring for a bridal gift
    When my home-bound pennant flies?
The rarest that be on land or sea
    It shall be my lady's prize,"

" There's never a prize on sea or land
    Could bring such joy to me
As my true love sound and homeward bound
    With a king's ship under his lee."

The Western ocean is wide and deep,
    And wild its tempests blow,
But bravely rides " Old Ironsides,"
    A-cruising to and fro.

We cruised to the east and we cruised to north,
   And southing far went we,
And at last off Cape de Verd we raised
   Two frigates sailing free.

Oh, God made man, and man made ships,
   But God makes very few
Like him who sailed our ship that day,
   And fought her, one to two.

He gained the weather-gage of both,
   He held them both a-lee;
And gun for gun, till set of sun,
   He spoke them fair and free;

Till the night-fog fell on spar and sail,
   And ship, and sea, and shore,
And our only aim was the bursting flame
   And the hidden cannon's roar.

Then a long rift in the mist showed up
   The stout *Cyane*, close-hauled
To swing in our wake and our quarter rake,
   And a boasting Briton bawled:

"Starboard and larboard, we've got him fast
   Where his heels won't take him through;
Let him luff or wear, he'll find us there, —
   Ho, Yankee, which will you do?"

THE CONSTITUTION'S LAST FIGHT.

We did not luff and we did not wear,
    But braced our topsails back,
Till the sternway drew us fair and true
    Broadsides athwart her track.

Athwart her track and across her bows
    We raked her fore and aft,
And out of the fight and into the night
    Drifted the beaten craft.

The slow *Levant* came up too late;
    No need had we to stir;
Her decks we swept with fire, and kept
    The flies from troubling her.

We raked her again, and her flag came down, —
    The haughtiest flag that floats, —
And the lime-juice dogs lay there like logs,
    With never a bark in their throats.

With never a bark and never a bite,
    But only an oath to break,
As we squared away for Praya Bay
    With our prizes in our wake.

Parole they gave and parole they broke,
    What matters the cowardly cheat,
If the captain's bride was satisfied
    With the one prize laid at her feet?

A Yankee ship and a Yankee crew —
   Constitution, where ye bound for?
Wherever the British prizes be,
Though it's one to two, or one to three, —
" Old Ironsides " means victory,
   Acrost the Western ocean.

                 —James Jeffrey Roche.

THE WAR WITH MEXICO

The Defence of the Alamo.

SANTA ANA came storming, as a storm might
come;
There was rumble of cannon; there was rattle of
blade;
There was cavalry, infantry, bugle, and drum, —
Full seven thousand, in pomp and parade,
The chivalry, flower of Mexico;
And a gaunt two hundred in the Alamo!

And thirty lay sick, and some were shot through;
For the siege had been bitter, and bloody, and
long.
"Surrender, or die!" — "Men, what will *you* do?"
And Travis, great Travis, drew sword, quick and
strong;
Drew a line at his feet . . . "Will you come? Will
you go?
I die with my wounded, in the Alamo."

The Bowie gasped, "Lead me over that line!"
Then Crockett, one hand to the sick, one hand to
his gun,
Crossed with him; then never a word or a sign
Till all, sick or well, all, all save but one,

One man.   Then a woman stepped, praying, and
    slow
Across ; to die at her post in the Alamo.

Then that one coward fled, in the night, in that night
    When all men silently prayed and thought
Of home ; of to-morrow ; of God and the right,
    Till dawn : and with dawn came Travis's cannon-
        shot,
In answer to insolent Mexico,
    From the old bell-tower of the Alamo.

Then came Santa Ana; a crescent of flame !
    Then the red " escalade ; " then the fight hand to
        hand ;
Such an unequal fight as never had name
    Since the Persian hordes butchered that doomed
        Spartan band.
All day, — all day and all night, and the morning ? so
    slow
Through the battle smoke mantling the Alamo.

Now silence ! Such silence ! Two thousand lay dead
    In a crescent outside ! And within? Not a breath
Save the gasp of a woman, with gory gashed head,
    All alone, all alone there, waiting for death ;
And she but a nurse.   Yet when shall we know
    Another like this of the Alamo?

THE DEFENCE OF THE ALAMO.

Shout " Victory, victory, victory ho ! "
    I say 'tis not always to the hosts that win;
I say that the victory, high or low,
    Is given the hero who grapples with sin,
Or legion or single ; just asking to know
    When duty fronts death in his Alamo.

                    —*Joaquin Miller.*

Monterey.

WE were not many, — we who stood
    Before the iron sleet that day ;
Yet many a gallant spirit would
Give half his years if but he could
    Have with us been at Monterey.

Now here, now there, the shot it hail'd
    In deadly drifts of fiery spray,
Yet not a single soldier quail'd
When wounded comrades round them wail'd
    Their dying shout at Monterey.

And on — still on our column kept
    Through walls of flame its withering way ;
Where fell the dead, the living stept,
Still charging on the guns which swept
    The slippery streets of Monterey.

The foe himself recoil'd aghast,
    When, striking where the strongest lay,
We swoop'd his flanking batteries past,
And braving full their murderous blast,
    Storm'd home the towers of Monterey.

MONTEREY.

Our banners on those turrets wave,
   And there our evening bugles play:
Where orange-boughs above their grave
Keep green the memory of the brave
   Who fought and fell at Monterey.

We are not many, — we who press'd
   Beside the brave who fell that day, —
But who of us has not confess'd
He'd rather share their warrior rest
   Than not have been at Monterey?

             — *Charles Fenno Hoffman.*

Buena Vista.

FROM the Rio Grande's waters to the icy lakes of
    Maine,
Let all exult! for we have met the enemy again;
Beneath their stern old mountains we have met them
    in their pride,
And rolled from Buena Vista back the battle's bloody
    tide;
Where the enemy came surging swift, like the Missis-
    sippi's flood,
And the reaper, Death, with strong arms swung his
    sickle red with blood.

Santana boasted loudly that, before two hours were
    past,
His Lancers through Saltillo should pursue us fierce
    and fast: —
On comes his solid infantry, line marching after line;
Lo! their great standards in the sun like sheets of
    silver shine:
With thousands upon thousands, — yea, with more
    than three to one, —
Their forests of bright bayonets fierce-flashing in the
    sun.

Lo! Guanajuato's regiment; Morelos's boasted corps,
And Guadalajara's chosen troops!— all veterans tried
    before.
Lo! galloping upon the right four thousand lances
    gleam,
Where, floating in the morning wind, their blood-red
    pennons stream;
And here his stern artillery climbs up the broad pla-
    teau:
To-day he means to strike at us an overwhelming
    blow.

Now, Wool, hold strongly to the heights! for lo! the
    mighty tide
Comes, thundering like an avalanche, deep, terrible,
    and wide.
Now, Illinois, stand steady! Now, Kentucky, to
    their aid!
For a portion of our line, alas! is broken and dis-
    mayed:
Great bands of shameless fugitives are fleeing from
    the field,
And the day is lost, if Illinois and brave Kentucky
    yield.

One of O'Brien's guns is gone!— On, on their masses
    drift,
Till their cavalry and infantry outflank us on the left;

Our light troops, driven from the hills, retreat in wild
  dismay,
And round us gather, thick and dark, the Mexican
  array.
Santana thinks the day is gained; for, now approach-
  ing near,
Miñon's dark cloud of Lancers sternly menaces our
  rear.

Now, Lincoln, gallant gentleman, lies dead upon the
  field,
Who strove to stay those cravens, when before the
  storm they reeled.
Fire, Washington, fire fast and true! Fire, Sherman,
  fast and far!
Lo! Bragg comes thundering to the front, to breast
  the adverse war!
Santana thinks the day is gained! On, on his masses
  crowd,
And the roar of battle swells again more terrible and
  loud.

Not yet! Our brave old general comes to regain the
  day;
Kentucky, to the rescue! Mississippi, to the fray!
Again our line advances! Gallant Davis fronts the
  foe,

And back before his rifles, in red waves, the Lancers
    flow.
Upon them yet once more, ye brave! The avalanche
    is stayed!
Back roll the Aztec multitudes, all broken and dis-
    mayed.

Ride, May! — To Buena Vista! for the Lancers gain
    our rear,
And we have few troops there to check their vehe-
    ment career.
Charge, Arkansas! Kentucky, charge! Yell, Porter,
    Vaughan, are slain,
But the shattered troops cling desperately unto that
    crimsoned plain;
Till, with the Lancers intermixed, pursuing and pur-
    sued,
Westward, in combat hot and close, drifts off the
    multitude.

And May comes charging from the hills with his
    ranks of flaming steel,
While shattered with a sudden fire, the foe already
    reel:
They flee amain! — Now to the left, to stay the tor-
    rent there,
Or else the day is surely lost, in horror and despair!

For their hosts pour swiftly onward, like a river in
    the spring,
Our flank is turned, and on our left their cannon
    thundering.

Now, good Artillery! bold Dragoons! Steady, brave
    hearts, be calm!
Through rain, cold hail, and thunder, now nerve each
    gallant arm!
What though their shot fall round us here, yet thicker
    than the hail?
We'll stand against them, as the rock stands firm
    against the gale.
Lo! their battery is silenced! but our iron sleet still
    showers:
They falter, halt, retreat! — Hurrah! the glorious day
    is ours!

In front, too, has the fight gone well, where upon gal-
    lant Lane,
And on stout Mississippi, the thick Lancers charged
    in vain:
Ah! brave Third Indiana! you have nobly wiped
    away
The reproach that through another corps befell your
    State to-day;

For back, all broken and dismayed, before your storm
    of fire,
Santana's boasted chivalry, a shattered wreck, retire.

Now charge again, Santana! or the day is surely
    lost, —
For back, like broken waves, along our left your
    hordes are tossed.
Still faster roar his batteries, — his whole reserve
    moves on ;
More work remains for us to do, ere the good fight is
    won.
Now for your wives and children, men! Stand steady
    yet once more!
Fight for your lives and honors! Fight as you never
    fought before!

Ho! Hardin breasts it bravely! and heroic Bissell
    there
Stands firm before the storm of balls that fill the as-
    tonished air :
The Lancers dash upon them, too! The foe swarm
    ten to one :
Hardin is slain; McKee and Clay the last time see
    the sun ;
And many another gallant heart, in that last desper-
    ate fray,

Grew cold, its last thought turning to its loved ones
    far away.

Speed, speed, Artillery! to the front!—for the hurri-
    cane of fire
Crushes those noble regiments, reluctant to retire!
Speed swiftly! Gallop! Ah! they come! Again
    Bragg climbs the ridge,
And his grape sweeps down the swarming foe, as a
    strong man moweth sedge;
Thus baffled in their last attack, compelled perforce
    to yield,
Still menacing in firm array, their columns leave the
    field.

The guns still roared at intervals; but silence fell at
    last,
And on the dead and dying came the evening shad-
    ows fast.
And then above the mountains rose the cold moon's
    silver shield,
And patiently and pitying she looked upon the field.
While careless of his wounded, and neglectful of his
    dead,
Despairingly and sullenly by night Santana fled.

And thus on Buena Vista's heights a long day's work
    was done,

BUENA VISTA.

And thus our brave old general another battle won.
Still, still our glorious banner waves, unstained by
      flight or shame,
And the Mexicans among their hills still tremble at
      our name.
So, honor unto those that stood!   Disgrace to those
      that fled!
And everlasting glory unto Buena Vista's dead!

—Albert Pike.

The Bivouac of the Dead.

THE muffled drum's sad roll has beat
　　The soldier's last tattoo !
No more on life's parade shall meet
　　That brave and fallen few.
On Fame's eternal camping-ground
　　Their silent tents are spread ;
And Glory guards, with solemn round,
　　The bivouac of the dead.

No rumor of the foe's advance
　　Now swells upon the wind ;
No troubled thought at midnight haunts
　　Of loved ones left behind ;
No vision of the morrow's strife
　　The warrior's dream alarms,
No braying horn, or screaming fife
　　At dawn shall call to arms.

Their shivered swords are red with rust,
　　Their plumèd heads are bowed ;
Their haughty banner, trailed in dust,
　　Is now their martial shroud ;
And plenteous funeral tears have washed
　　The red stains from each brow ;

And the proud forms, by battle gashed,
  Are free from anguish now.

The neighing troop, the flashing blade,
  The bugle's stirring blast,
The charge, the dreadful cannonade,
  The din and shout, are passed;
Nor war's wild note, nor glory's peal,
  Shall thrill with fierce delight
Those breasts that nevermore may feel
  The rapture of the fight.

Like the fierce Northern hurricane
  That sweeps his great plateau,
Flushed with the triumph yet to gain
  Came down the serried foe.
Who heard the thunder of the fray
  Break o'er the field beneath,
Knew well the watchword of that day
  Was "Victory or death."

Full many a norther's breath has swept
  O'er Angostura's plain,
And long the pitying sky has wept
  Above its mouldered slain.
The raven's scream, or eagle's flight,
  Or shepherd's pensive lay,

Alone awakes each sullen height
   That frowned o'er that dark fray.

Sons of the Dark and Bloody Ground,
   Ye must not slumber there,
Where stranger steps and tongues resound,
   Along the heedless air;
Your own proud land's heroic soil
   Shall be your fitter grave;
She claims from war his richest spoil,
   The ashes of her brave.

Thus 'neath their parent turf they rest,
   Far from the gory field,
Borne to a Spartan mother's breast
   On many a bloody shield.
The sunshine of their native sky
   Smiles sadly on them here,
And kindred eyes and hearts watch by
   The heroes' sepulchre.

Rest on, embalmed and sainted dead!
   Dear as the blood ye gave,
No impious footstep here shall tread
   The herbage of your grave.
Nor shall your story be forgot
   While Fame her record keeps,

THE BIVOUAC OF THE DEAD.

Or Honor points the hallowed spot
    Where Valor proudly sleeps.

Yon marble minstrel's voiceless stone
    In deathless song shall tell,
When many a vanished age hath flown,
    The story how ye fell;
Nor wreck, nor change, nor winter's blight,
    Nor time's remorseless doom,
Shall dim one ray of glory's light
    That gilds your deathless tomb.

— Theodore O'Hara.

THE CIVIL WAR

Brother Jonathan's Lament for Sister Caroline.

Written in December, 1860, when South Carolina adopted the Ordinance of Secession.

SHE has gone, — she has left us in passion and
    pride, —
Our stormy-browed sister, so long at our side !
She has torn her own star from our firmament's glow,
And turned on her brother the face of a foe !

O Caroline, Caroline, child of the sun,
We can never forget that our hearts have been one, —
Our foreheads both sprinkled in Liberty's name,
From the fountain of blood with the finger of flame !

You were always too ready to fire at a touch;
But we said: "She's a beauty, — she does not mean
    much."
We have scowled when you uttered some turbulent
    threat;
But Friendship still whispered: "Forgive and for-
    get."

Has our love all died out? Have its altars grown
    cold?

Has the curse come at last which the fathers fore-
    told?
Then Nature must teach us the strength of the chain
That her petulant children would sever in vain.

They may fight till the buzzards are gorged with their
    spoil,
Till the harvest grows black as it rots in the soil,
Till the wolves and the catamounts troop from their
    caves,
And the shark tracks the pirate, the lord of the
    waves:

In vain is the strife!   When its fury is past,
Their fortunes must flow in one channel at last,
As the torrents that rush from the mountains of snow
Roll mingled in peace in the valleys below.

Our Union is river, lake, ocean, and sky;
Man breaks not the medal when God cuts the die!
Though darkened with sulphur, though cloven with
    steel,
The blue arch will brighten, the waters will heal!

O Caroline, Caroline, child of the sun,
There are battles with fate that can never be won!
The star-flowering banner must never be furled,
For its blossoms of light are the hope of the world!

BROTHER JONATHAN'S LAMENT.

Go, then, our rash sister, afar and aloof, —
Run wild in the sunshine away from our roof ;
But when your heart aches, and your feet have
    grown sore,
Remember the pathway that leads to our door !

          — *Oliver Wendell Holmes.*

Men of the North and West.

Published in the *World* after the fall of Fort Sumter.

MEN of the North and West,
    Wake in your might.
Prepare, as the rebels have done,
    For the fight !
You cannot shrink from the test ;
Rise !　Men of the North and West !

They have torn down your banner of stars ;
    They have trampled the laws ;
They have stifled the freedom they hate,
    For no cause !
Do you love it or slavery best ?
Speak !　Men of the North and West !

They strike at the life of the State :
    Shall the murder be done ?
They cry : " We are two ! "　And you ?
    " We are one ! "
You must meet them, then, breast to breast ;
On !　Men of the North and West !

MEN OF THE NORTH AND WEST.

Not with words; they laugh them to scorn,
    And tears they despise;
But with swords in your hands, and death
    In your eyes!
Strike home! leave to God all the rest;
Strike! Men of the North and West!

       — Richard Henry Stoddard.

No More Words.

NO more words;
　　Try it with your swords!
Try it with the arms of your bravest and your
　　best!
You are proud of your manhood, now put it to
　　the test;
　　　Not another word;
　　　Try it by the sword!

　　　No more notes;
　　　Try it by the throats
Of the cannon that will roar till the earth and
　　air be shaken;
For they speak what they mean, and they can-
　　not be mistaken;
　　　No more doubt;
　　　Come, — fight it out!

　　　No child's play!
　　　Waste not a day;
Serve out the deadliest weapons that you know;
Let them pitilessly hail on the faces of the foe;
　　　No blind strife;
　　　Waste not one life.

NO MORE WORDS.

You that in the front
Bear the battle's brunt —
When the sun gleams at dawn on the bayonets
    abreast,
Remember 'tis for government and country you
    contest;
    For love of all you guard,
    Stand, and strike hard!

You at home that stay
From danger far away,
Leave not a jot to chance, while you rest in
    quiet ease;
Quick! forge the bolts of death; quick! ship
    them o'er the seas;
    If War's feet are lame,
    Yours will be the blame.

You, my lads, abroad,
" Steady ! " be your word ;
You, at home, be the anchor of your soldiers
    young and brave ;
Spare no cost, none is lost, that may strengthen
    or may save ;
    Sloth were sin and shame ;
    Now play out the game !

                 — *Franklin Lushington.*

The Troop-ship Sails.

IT is good-by,
       My lad?
No, I'll not cry.
Has the time come?
The bugle-call from the sea-wall,
The tap of drum?
My tears are dry.

Rest your head here,
       My lad,
Close to me, dear;
Why do you stare?
Have pain and care made me less fair?
Are my lips white with fear?
Hark! how they cheer
Down in the Square there!

What do they care,
       My lad,
For this brown hair
That I love so?
Their drums' long roll will crush my
       soul —
Ah, God! don't go! —
I cannot bear —

THE TROOP-SHIP SAILS.

There, I'll be still,
  My lad,
Truly I will;
My tears are spent.
Which regiment will next be sent?
Does every bullet kill?
Hold me until
The call is urgent!

Who spoke your name,
  My lad?
The summons came
Out of the crowd!
Oh, hold me, lad! fold me, lad!
Their flag's a shroud
To bury shame!

Have they begun,
  My lad?
See, the troops run!
Your eyes are wet;
You are so quiet; is there time yet?
God! it's the signal gun!
Kiss me, — just one.
Run with your musket!
              — *R. W. Chambers.*

The Stripes and the Stars.

O STAR-SPANGLED banner! the flag of our
    pride!
Though trampled by traitors and basely defied,
Fling out to the glad winds your red, white, and blue,
For the heart of the Northland is beating for you!
And her strong arm is nerving to strike with a will,
Till the foe and his boastings are humbled and still!
Here's welcome to wounding and combat and scars
And the glory of death — for the Stripes and the
    Stars!

From prairie, O ploughman! speed boldly away, —
There's seed to be sown in God's furrows to-day!
Row landward, lone fisher! stout woodman, come
    home!
Let smith leave his anvil and weaver his loom,
And hamlet and city ring loud with the cry:
" For God and our country we'll fight till we die!
Here's welcome to wounding and combat and scars
And the glory of death — for the Stripes and the
    Stars!"

Invincible banner! the flag of the free,
Oh, where treads the foot that would falter for thee?

THE STRIPES AND THE STARS.

Or the hands to be folded, till triumph is won
And the eagle looks proud, as of old, to the sun?
Give tears for the parting — a murmur of prayer —
Then forward ! the fame of our standard to share !
With welcome to wounding and combat and scars
And the glory of death — for the Stripes and the
      Stars !

O God of our fathers ! this banner must shine
Where battle is hottest, in warfare divine !
The cannon has thundered, the bugle has blown —
We fear not the summons — we fight not alone !
Oh, lead us, till wide from the gulf to the sea
The land shall be sacred to freedom and thee !
With love for oppression ; with blessing for scars —
One country — one banner — the Stripes and the
      Stars !

              — *Edna Dean Proctor.*

Spring at the Capital.

THE poplar drops beside the way
  Its tasselled plumes of silver gray;
The chestnut points its great brown buds, impatient
  for the laggard May.

The honeysuckles lace the wall;
The hyacinths grow fair and tall;
And mellow sun, and pleasant wind, and odorous
  bees are over all.

Down-looking in this snow-white bud,
How distant seems the war's red flood!
How far remote the streaming wounds, the sickening
  scent of human blood!

For Nature does not recognize
This strife that rends the earth and skies;
No war-dreams vex the winter's sleep of clover-heads
  and daisy-eyes.

She holds her even way the same,
Though navies sink, or cities flame;
A snowdrop is a snowdrop still, despite the Nation's
  joy or shame.

SPRING AT THE CAPITAL.

When blood her grassy altar wets,
She sends the pitying violets
To heal the outrage with their bloom, and cover it
    with soft regrets.

O crocuses with rain-wet eyes,
O tender-lipped anemones,
What do you know of agony, and death, and blood-
    won victories?

No shudder breaks your sunshine trance,
Though near you rolls, with slow advance,
Clouding your shining leaves with dust, the anguish-
    laden ambulance.

Yonder a white encampment hums;
The clash of martial music comes;
And now your startled stems are all a-tremble with
    the jar of drums.

Whether it lessen or increase,
Or whether trumpets shout or cease,
Still, deep within your tranquil hearts, the happy bees
    are humming, " Peace !"

O flowers ! the soul that faints or grieves
New comfort from your lips receives;
Sweet confidence and patient faith are hidden in your
    healing leaves.

Help us to trust still on and on,
That this dark night will soon be gone,
And that these battle-stains are but the blood-red
trouble of the dawn, —

Dawn of a broader, whiter day
Than ever blessed us with its ray, —
A dawn beneath whose purer light all guilt and
wrong shall fade away.

Then shall our Nation break its bands,
And, silencing the envious lands,
Stand in the searching light unshamed, with spotless
robe, and clean, white hands.

— *Elizabeth Akers Allen.*

Roll=call.

"CORPORAL GREEN!" the orderly cried.
  "Here!" was the answer, loud and clear,
  From the lips of the soldier who stood near;
And "Here!" was the word the next replied.

"Cyrus Drew!"— then a silence fell,—
  This time no answer followed the call;
  Only his rear man had seen him fall,
Killed or wounded, he could not tell.

There they stood in the failing light,
  These men of battle with grave, dark looks,
  As plain to be read as open books,
While slowly gathered the shades of night.

The fern on the hillsides was splashed with blood,
  And down in the corn, where the poppies grew,
  Were redder stains than the poppies knew;
And crimson-dyed was the river's flood.

For the foe had crossed from the other side
  That day, in the face of a murderous fire
  That swept them down in its terrible ire,
And their life-blood went to color the tide.

133

" Herbert Kline ! "   At the call there came
  Two stalwart soldiers into the line,
  Bearing between them this Herbert Kline,
Wounded and bleeding, to answer his name.

" Ezra Kerr ! "— and a voice answered, " Here ! "
  " Hiram Kerr ! " — but no man replied.
  They were brothers, these two ; the sad wind
      sighed,
And a shudder crept through the corn-field near.

" Ephraim Deane ! " — then a soldier spoke :
  " Deane carried our regiment colors," he said ;
  " Where our ensign was shot, I left him dead,
Just after the enemy wavered and broke.

" Close to the roadside his body lies ;
  I paused a moment and gave him drink ;
  He murmured his mother's name, I think,
And Death came with it, and closed his eyes."

'Twas a victory, yes, but it cost us dear, —
  For that company's roll, when called at night,
  Of a hundred men who went into the fight,
Numbered but twenty that answered, " Here ! "

                    — *Nathaniel G. Shepherd.*

The Reveille.

HARK! I hear the tramp of thousands,
    And of armèd men the hum;
Lo! a nation's hosts have gathered
    Round the quick-alarming drum
        Saying, " Come,
        Freemen, come!
Ere your heritage be wasted," said the quick-alarm-
ing drum.

" Let me of my heart take counsel:
    War is not of life the sum;
Who shall stay and reap the harvest
    When the autumn days shall come?"
        But the drum
        Echoed, " Come!
Death shall reap the braver harvest," said the sol-
emn-sounding drum.

" But when won the coming battle,
    What of profit springs therefrom?
What if conquest, subjugation,
    Even greater ills become?
        But the drum
        Answered, " Come!

You must do the sum to prove it," said the Yankee-
answering drum.

" What if, 'mid the cannon's thunder,
    Whistling shot, and bursting bomb,
When my brothers fall around me,
    Should my heart grow cold and numb?"
            But the drum
            Answered, " Come!
Better there in death united, than in life a recreant
    — Come!"

Thus they answered, — hoping, fearing,
    Some in faith, and doubting some, —
Till a trumpet-voice, proclaiming,
    Said, " My chosen people, come!"
            Then the drum,
            Lo! was dumb;
For the great heart of the nation, throbbing, an-
    swered, "Lord, we come!"

                                    — *Bret Harte.*

The Cumberland.

AT anchor in Hampton Roads we lay,
　　On board of the *Cumberland* sloop-of-war;
And at times from the fortress across the bay
　　The alarum of drums swept past,
　　Or a bugle-blast
From the camp on the shore.

Then far away to the south uprose
　　A little feather of snow-white smoke,
And we knew that the iron ship of our foes
　　Was steadily steering its course
　　To try the force
Of our ribs of oak.

Down upon us heavily runs,
　　Silent and sullen, the floating fort;
Then comes a puff of smoke from her guns,
　　And leaps the terrible death,
　　With fiery breath,
From each open port.

We are not idle, but send her straight
　　Defiance back in a full broadside!
As hail rebounds from a roof of slate,

Rebounds our heavier hail
From each iron scale
Of the monster's hide.

" Strike your flag ! " the rebel cries,
In his arrogant old plantation strain.
" Never ! " our gallant Morris replies :
" It is better to sink than to yield ! "
And the whole air pealed
With the cheers of our men.

Then like a kraken huge and black,
She crushed our ribs in her iron grasp !
Down went the *Cumberland* all awrack,
With a sudden shudder of death,
And the cannon's breath
For her dying gasp.

Next morn, as the sun rose over the bay,
Still floated our flag at the mainmast-head.
Lord, how beautiful was thy day !
Every waft of the air
Was a whisper of prayer,
Or a dirge for the dead.

Ho ! brave hearts that went down in the seas !
Ye are at peace in the troubled stream.
Ho ! brave land ! with hearts like these,

THE CUMBERLAND.

Thy flag, that is rent in twain,
Shall be one again,
And without a seam.

— Henry Wadsworth Longfellow.

The Banner of the Stars.

HURRAH! boys, hurrah! fling our banner to the
breeze!
Let the enemies of freedom see its folds again
unfurled.
And down with the pirates that scorn upon the seas
Our victorious Yankee banner, sign of Freedom
to the World!

CHORUS.

We'll never have a new flag, for ours is the true flag,
The true flag, the true flag, the Red, White, and
Blue flag.
Hurrah! boys, hurrah! we will carry to the wars
The old flag, the free flag, the Banner of the Stars.

And what tho' its white shall be crimsoned with our
blood?
And what tho' its stripes shall be shredded in the
storms?
To the torn flag, the worn flag, we'll keep our promise
good,
And we'll bear the starry blue field, with gallant
hearts and arms. — CHO.

Then, cursed be he who would strike our Starry
    Flag!
  May the God of Hosts be with us, as we smite the
    traitor down !
And cursed be he who would hesitate or lag
  Till the dear flag, the fair flag, with Victory we
    crown. — CHO.

— R. W. Raymond.

When This Cruel War Is Over.

DEAREST love, do you remember
  When we last did meet,
How you told me that you loved me
  Kneeling at my feet?
Oh, how proud you stood before me
  In your suit of blue,
When you vowed to me and country
  Ever to be true.

CHORUS.

Weeping sad and lonely,
Hopes and fears how vain!
Yet praying,
When this cruel war is over,
Praying that we meet again.

When the summer breeze is sighing
  Mournfully along,
Or when autumn leaves are falling,
  Sadly breathes the song.
Oft in dreams I see thee lying
  On the battle plain,
Lonely, wounded, even dying,
  Calling, but in vain. — CHO.

142

WHEN THIS CRUEL WAR IS OVER.

If, amid the din of battle,
   Nobly you should fall,
Far away from those who love you,
   None to hear you call,
Who would whisper words of comfort,
   Who would soothe your pain?
Ah, the many cruel fancies
   Ever in my brain! — CHO.

But our country called you, darling,
   Angels cheer your way!
While our nation's sons are fighting,
   We can only pray.
Nobly strike for God and country,
   Let all nations see
How we love the starry banner,
   Emblem of the free. — CHO.

              — *Charles Carroll Sawyer.*

Tramp, Tramp, Tramp.

IN the prison cell I sit,
  Thinking, mother dear, of you,
And our bright and happy home so far away,
  And the tears they fill my eyes,
  Spite of all that I can do,
Tho' I try to cheer my comrades and be gay.

CHORUS.

Tramp, tramp, tramp, the boys are marching,
  Oh, cheer up, comrades, they will come,
And beneath the starry flag we shall breathe the air
    again,
  Of freedom in our own beloved home.

In the battle front we stood
  When the fiercest charge they made,
And they swept us off a hundred men or more,
  But before we reached their lines
  They were beaten back dismayed,
And we heard the cry of vict'ry o'er and o'er. — Cho.

So, within the prison cell,
  We are waiting for the day

That shall come to open wide the iron door,
   And the hollow eye grows bright,
   And the poor heart almost gay,
As we think of seeing friends and home once more.
— Cho.
— George F. Root.

Marching Along.

THE army is gathering from near and from far;
  The trumpet is sounding the call for the war;
McClellan's our leader, he's gallant and strong;
We'll gird on our armor and be marching along.

CHORUS.

Marching along, we are marching along,
Gird on the armor and be marching along;
McClellan's our leader, he's gallant and strong;
For God and our country we are marching along.

The foe is before us in battle array,
But let us not waver, or turn from the way;
The Lord is our strength, and the Union's our song;
With courage and faith we are marching along.
                                    — CHO.

Our wives and our children we leave in your care,
We feel you will help them with sorrow to bear;
'Tis hard thus to part, but we hope 'twon't be long;
We'll keep up our heart as we're marching along.
                                    — CHO.

MARCHING ALONG.

We sigh for our country, we mourn for our dead;
For them now our last drop of blood we will shed;
Our cause is the right one, — our foe's in the wrong;
Then gladly we'll sing as we're marching along.
                                                — CHO.

The flag of our country is floating on high;
We'll stand by that flag till we conquer or die;
McClellan's our leader, he's gallant and strong;
We'll gird on our armor and be marching along.
                                                — CHO.
                              — *William B. Bradbury.*

The Blue and the Gray.

BY the flow of the inland river,
  Whence the fleets of iron had fled,
Where the blades of the grave-grass quiver,
  Asleep are the ranks of the dead, —
    Under the sod and the dew;
      Waiting the judgment day;
    Under the one, the Blue;
      Under the other, the Gray.

These in the robings of glory,
  Those in the gloom of defeat;
All with the battle-blood gory,
  In the dusk of eternity meet, —
    Under the sod and the dew;
      Waiting the judgment day;
    Under the laurel, the Blue;
      Under the willow, the Gray.

From the silence of sorrowful hours
  The desolate mourners go,
Lovingly laden with flowers,
  Alike for the friend and the foe;
    Under the sod and the dew;
      Waiting the judgment day;

THE BLUE AND THE GRAY.

Under the roses, the Blue;
Under the lilies, the Gray.

So, with an equal splendor,
The morning sun-rays fall,
With a touch impartially tender,
On the blossoms blooming for all, —
Under the sod and the dew;
Waiting the judgment day;
Broidered with gold, the Blue;
Mellowed with gold, the Gray.

So, when the summer calleth
On forest, and field of grain,
With an equal murmur falleth
The cooling drip of the rain;
Under the sod and the dew;
Waiting the judgment day;
Wet with the rain, the Blue;
Wet with the rain, the Gray.

Sadly, but not with upbraiding,
The generous deed was done;
In the storm of the years now fading
No braver battle was won;
Under the sod and the dew;
Waiting the judgment day;

Under the blossoms, the Blue;
Under the garlands, the Gray.

No more shall the war cry sever,
Or the winding rivers be red;
They banish our anger forever
When they laurel the graves of our dead.
Under the sod and the dew;
Waiting the judgment day;
Love and tears for the Blue;
Tears and love for the Gray.

— Francis M. Finch.

𝕿𝖍𝖊 𝕾𝖒𝖆𝖑𝖑𝖊𝖘𝖙 𝖔𝖋 𝖙𝖍𝖊 𝕯𝖗𝖚𝖒𝖘.

WHEN the opulence of summer unto wood and
    meadow comes,
  And within the tangled graveyard riot old-time
    spice and bloom,
Then dear Nature brings her tribute to the " smallest
    of the drums,"
  Spreads the sweetest of her blossoms on the little
    soldier's tomb.

In the quiet country village, still they tell you how
    he died;
  And the story moves you strangely, more than
    other tales of war.
Thrice heroic seems the hero, if he be a child
    beside,
  And the wound that tears his bosom is more sad
    than others far.

In the ranks of Sherman's army none so young and
    small as he,
  With his face so soft and dimpled, and his inno-
    cent blue eyes.
Yet of all the Union drummers he could drum most
    skilfully,

With a spirit — said his colonel — fit to make the
  dead arise!

In the charge at Chickamauga (so, beside his little
  grave,
  You may learn the hero's story of some villager,
  perchance),
When his regiment sank, broken, from the rampart,
  like a wave,
  Thrice the clangor of his drum-beat rallied to a
  fresh advance.

There he stood upon the hillside, capless, with his
  shining hair
  Blown about his childish forehead like the bright
  silk of the corn;
And the men looked up, and saw him standing brave
  and scathless there,
  As an angel on a hilltop, in the drifting mist of
  morn.

Thrice they rallied at his drum - beat, — then the
  tattered flag went down!
  Some one caught it, waved it skyward for a moment, and then fell.
In the dust, and gore, and drabble, all the stars of
  freedom's crown,
  And the soldiers beaten backward from the emblem loved so well!

THE SMALLEST OF THE DRUMS.

Then our drummer-boy, our hero, from his neck the
    drum-cord flung,
  And amid the hail of bullets to the fallen banner
    sped.
Quick he raised it from dishonor; quick before
    them all he sprung,
  And in fearless, proud defiance, waved the old flag
    o'er his head !

For a minute's space the cheering, louder than the
    singing balls,
  And the soldiers pressing forward, closing up their
    broken line,
Then the child's bright head, death-stricken, on his
    throbbing bosom falls,
  And the brave eyes that God lighted cease with
    life and soul to shine.

In the flag he saved they wrapped him; in that
    starry shroud he lies,
  And the roses, and the lilacs, and the daisies seem
    to know ;
For in all that peaceful acre, sleeping 'neath the
    summer skies,
  There is neither mound nor tablet that is wreathed
    and guarded so !

—James Buckham.

Keenan's Charge.

THE sun had set;
　The leaves with dew were wet, —
Down fell a bloody dusk
Where Stonewall's corps, like a beast of prey,
Tore through with angry tusk.

" They've trapped us, boys!"
Rose from our flank a voice.
With a rush of steel and smoke
On came the rebels straight,
Eager as love, and wild as hate;
And our line reeled and broke;

Broke and fled.
Not one stayed, — but the dead!
With curses, shrieks, and cries,
Horses, and wagons, and men,
Tumbled back through the shuddering glen,
And above us the fading skies.

There's some hope, still, —
Those batteries parked on the hill!
" Battery, wheel " ('mid the roar),

KEENAN'S CHARGE.

" Pass pieces; fix prolonge to fire
Retiring.   Trot!"   In the panic dire
A bugle rings " Trot! "— and no more.

The horses plunged,
The cannon lurched and lunged,
To join the hopeless rout.
But suddenly rose a form
Calmly in front of the human storm.
With a stern, commanding shout :

" Align those guns!"
(We knew it was Pleasanton's.)
The cannoneers bent to obey,
And worked with a will at his word,
And the black guns moved as if they had heard.
But, ah, the dread delay !

" To wait is crime;
O God, for ten minutes' time!"
The general looked around.
There Keenan sat, like a stone,
With his three hundred horse alone,
Less shaken than the ground.

" Major, your men?"
" Are soldiers, general."   " Then,
Charge, major!   Do your best;

Hold the enemy back, at all cost,
Till my guns are placed; — else the army is
     lost.
You die to save the rest!"

By the shrouded gleam of the western skies
Brave Keenan looked into Pleasanton's eyes
For an instant, — clear, and cool, and still;
Then, with a smile, he said: "I will."

"Cavalry, charge!" Not a man of them
     shrank.
Their sharp, full cheer, from rank on rank,
Rose joyously, with a willing breath, —
Rose like a greeting hail to death.

Then forward they sprang, and spurred, and
     clashed;
Shouted the officers, crimson-sashed;
Rode well the men, each brave as his fellow,
In their faded coats of the blue and yellow;
And above in the air, with an instinct true,
Like a bird of war their pennon flew.

With clank of scabbard, and thunder of
     steeds,
And blades that shine like sunlit reeds,

And strong brown faces bravely pale
For fear their proud attempt shall fail,
Three hundred Pennsylvanians close
On twice ten thousand gallant foes.

Line after line the troopers came
To the edge of the wood that was ringed
        with flame;
Rode in, and sabred, and shot, — and fell;
Nor came one back his wounds to tell.
And full in the midst rose Keenan, tall,
In the gloom like a martyr awaiting his fall,
While the circle-stroke of his sabre, swung
'Round his head, like a halo there, luminous
    hung.

Line after line, ay, whole platoons,
Struck dead in their saddles, of brave dra-
        goons,
By the maddened horses were onward borne,
And into the vortex flung, trampled and torn;
As Keenan fought with his men, side by side.
So they rode, till there were no more to ride.

And over them, lying there shattered and
        mute,
What deep echo rolls? — 'Tis a death-salute

From the cannon in place; for, heroes, you
    braved
Your fate not in vain; the army was saved!

Over them now, — year following year, —
Over their graves the pine cones fall, ·
And the whippoorwill chants his spectre call;
But they stir not again, they raise no cheer;
They have ceased. But their glory shall
    never cease,
Nor their light be quenched in the light of
    peace.
The rush of their charge is resounding still
That saved the army at Chancellorsville.

                — *George Parsons Lathrop*.

Marching Through Georgia.

BRING the good old bugle, boys! we'll sing an
other song, —
Sing it with a spirit that will start the world along, —
Sing it as we used to sing it, fifty thousand strong,
While we were marching through Georgia.

CHORUS.

Hurrah, hurrah! we bring the jubilee!
Hurrah, hurrah! the flag that makes you free!
So we sang the chorus from Atlanta to the sea,
While we were marching through Georgia.

How the darkies shouted when they heard the joyful
sound!
How the turkeys gobbled which our commissary
found!
How the sweet potatoes even started from the ground,
While we were marching through Georgia! — CHO.

Yes, and there were Union men who wept with joyful
tears
When they saw the honor'd flag they had not seen
for years;

Hardly could they be restrained from breaking forth
    in cheers
While we were marching through Georgia. — CHO.

" Sherman's dashing Yankee boys will never reach
    the coast ! "
So the saucy rebels said, — and t'was a handsome
    boast.
Had they not forgot, alas ! to reckon on a host,
While we were marching through Georgia. — CHO.

So we made a thoroughfare for Freedom and her
    train,
Sixty miles in latitude, three hundred to the main ;
Treason fled before us, for resistance was in vain,
While we were marching through Georgia. — CHO.

O Captain! My Captain!

On the Death of Lincoln.

O Captain! my Captain! our fearful trip is done,
    The ship has weather'd every rack, the prize we
      sought is won,
The port is near, the bells I hear, the people all
      exulting,
While follow eyes the steady keel, the vessel grim
      and daring;

      But, O heart! heart! heart!
        Oh, the bleeding drops of red,
      Where on the deck my Captain lies,
        Fallen cold and dead.

O Captain! my Captain! rise up and hear the bells;
Rise up, — for you the flag is flung, — for you the
      bugle trills,
For you bouquets and ribbon'd wreaths, — for you
      the shores a-crowding,
For you they call, the swaying mass, their eager faces
      turning;

      Here, Captain! dear father!
      This arm beneath your head!

It is some dream that on the deck
You've fallen cold and dead.

My Captain does not answer, his lips are pale and
still ;
My father does not feel my arm, he has no pulse nor
will ;
The ship is anchor'd safe and sound, its voyage closed
and done,
From fearful trip the victor ship comes in with object
won ;

Exult, O shores, and ring, O bells !
But I, with mournful tread,
Walk the deck my Captain lies,
Fallen cold and dead.
                                        — *Walt Whitman.*

Battle Hymn of the Republic.

MINE eyes have seen the glory of the coming
of the Lord;
He is trampling out the vintage where the grapes
of wrath are stored;
He hath loosed the fateful lightning of his terrible
swift sword;
His truth is marching on.

CHORUS.

Glory! Glory Hallelujah!
Glory! Glory Hallelujah!
Glory! Glory Hallelujah!
His truth is marching on.

I have seen him in the watch-fires of a hundred
circling camps;
They have builded him an altar in the evening dews
and damps;
I can read his righteous sentence by the dim and
flaring lamps;
His day is marching on. — Cho.

I have read a fiery gospel writ in burnished rows of
steel:

"As ye deal with my contemners, so with you my
    grace shall deal."
Let the hero born of woman crush the serpent with
    his heel,
        Since God is marching on. — CHO.

He has sounded forth the trumpet that shall never
    call retreat;
He is sifting out the hearts of men before his judg-
    ment seat;
Oh, be swift, my soul, to answer him; be jubilant,
    my feet;
        Our God is marching on. — CHO.

In the beauty of the lilies Christ was born across the
    sea,
With a glory in his bosom that transfigures you and
    me ;
As He died to make men holy, let us die to make
    men free,
        While God is marching on. — CHO.
                  —*Julia Ward Howe.*

Lyon.

SING, bird, on green Missouri's plain,
   Thy saddest song of sorrow;
Drop tears, O clouds, in gentlest rain
   Ye from the winds can borrow;
Breathe out, ye winds, your softest sigh,
   Weep, flowers, in dewy splendor,
For him who knew well how to die,
   But never to surrender!

Up rose serene the August sun
   Upon that day of glory;
Up curled from musket and from gun
   The war-cloud gray and hoary.
It gathered like a funeral pall
   Now broken and now blended,
Where rang the bugle's angry call,
   And rank with rank contended.

Four thousand men, as brave and true
   As e'er went forth in daring,
Upon the foe that morning threw
   The strength of their despairing.
They feared not death, — men bless the field
   That patriot soldiers die on, —

Fair Freedom's cause was sword and shield,
And at their head was Lyon!

The leader's troubled soul looked forth
From eyes of troubled brightness;
Sad soul! the burden of the North
Had pressed out all its lightness.
He gazed upon the unequal fight,
His ranks all rent and gory,
And felt the shadows close like night
Round his career of glory.

"General, come lead us!" loud the cry
From a brave band was ringing, —
"Lead us, and we will stop, or die,
That battery's awful singing."
He spurred to where his heroes stood,
Twice wounded, — no wound knowing, —
The fire of battle in his blood
And on his forehead glowing.

Oh, cursed for aye that traitor's hand,
And cursed that aim so deadly,
Which smote the bravest of the land,
And dyed his bosom redly!
Serene he lay, while past him prest
The battle's furious billow,

LYON.

As calmly as a babe may rest
  Upon its mother's pillow.

So Lyon died! and well may flowers
  His place of burial cover,
For never had this land of ours
  A more devoted lover.
Living, his country was his pride,
  His life he gave her, dying;
Life, fortune, love, — he naught denied
  To her and to her sighing.

Rest, patriot, in thy hillside grave,
  Beside her form who bore thee!
Long may the land thou diedst to save
  Her bannered stars wave o'er thee!
Upon her history's brightest page,
  And on Fame's glowing portal,
She'll write thy grand, heroic rage
  And grave thy name immortal.

                    — Henry Peterson.

The Fancy Shot.

"RIFLEMAN, shoot me a fancy shot,
   Straight at the heart of yon prowling vidette;
Ring me a ball in the glittering spot
   That shines on his breast like an amulet!"

"Ah, captain! here goes for a fine-drawn bead,
   There's music around when my barrel's in tune!"
Crack! went the rifle, the messenger sped,
   And dead from his horse fell the ringing dragoon.

"Now, rifleman, steal through the bushes, and
      snatch
   From your victim some trinket to handsel first
      blood;
A button, a loop, or that luminous patch
   That gleams in the moon like a diamond stud!"

"Oh, captain! I staggered and sunk on my track,
   When I gazed on the face of that fallen vidette,
For he looked so like you, as he lay on his back,
   That my heart rose upon me, and masters me yet.

"But I snatched off the trinket, — this locket of gold;
   An inch from the centre my lead broke its way,

THE FANCY SHOT.

Scarce grazing the picture, so fair to behold,
    Of a beautiful lady in bridal array."

" Ha! rifleman, fling me the locket! — 'tis she,
    My brother's young bride, — and the fallen dragoon
Was her husband — Hush! soldier, 'twas Heaven's
        decree,
    We must bury him there, by the light of the moon!

" But hark! the far bugles their warnings unite ;
    War is a virtue, weakness a sin ;
There's a lurking and loping around us to-night ; —
    Load again, rifleman, keep your hand in ! "
                 — *Charles Dawson Shanly.*

In the Hospital.

I LAY me down to sleep,
  With little thought or care
Whether my waking find
  Me here or there.

A bowing, burdened head,
That only asks to rest,
Unquestioning, upon
  A loving breast.

My good right hand forgets
Its cunning now.
To march the weary march
  I know not how.

I am not eager, bold,
Nor strong, — all that is past;
I am ready not to do
  At last, at last.

My half day's work is done,
And this is all my part;
I give a patient God
  My patient heart,

IN THE HOSPITAL.

And grasp his banner still,
Though all its blue be dim;
These stripes, no less than stars,
 Lead after him.

    — M. W. Howland.

Farragut.

FARRAGUT, Farragut,
  Old Heart of Oak,
Daring Dave Farragut,
  Thunderbolt stroke,
Watches the hoary mist
  Lift from the bay,
Till his flag, glory-kissed,
  Greets the young day.

Far, by gray Morgan's walls,
  Looms the black fleet.
Hark, deck to rampart calls
  With the drums' beat!
Buoy your chains overboard,
  While the steam hums;
Men! to the battlement,
  Farragut comes.

See, as the hurricane
  Hurtles in wrath
Squadrons of clouds amain
  Back from its path!
Back to the parapet,
  To the guns' lips,

FARRAGUT.

Thunderbolt Farragut
 Hurls the black ships.

Now through the battle's roar
 Clear the boy sings,
" By the mark fathoms four,"
 While his lead swings.
Steady the wheelmen five
 " Nor' by east keep her,"
" Steady," but two alive :
 How the shells sweep her !

Lashed to the mast that sways
 Over red decks,
Over the flame that plays
 Round the torn wrecks,
Over the dying lips
 Framed for a cheer,
Farragut leads his ships,
 Guides the line clear.

On by heights cannon-browed,
 While the spars quiver ;
Onward still flames the cloud
 Where the hulks shiver.
See, yon fort's star is set,
 Storm and fire past.

Cheer him, lads, — Farragut,
   Lashed to the mast !

Oh ! while Atlantic's breast
   Bears a white sail,
While the Gulf's towering crest
   Tops a green vale ;
Men thy bold deeds shall tell,
   Old Heart of Oak,
Daring Dave Farragut,
   Thunderbolt stroke !

*   — W. T. Meredith.*

John Burns of Gettysburg.

HAVE you heard the story that gossips tell
   Of Burns of Gettysburg? No? Ah, well:
Brief is the glory that hero earns,
Briefer the story of poor John Burns;
He was the fellow who won renown, —
The only man who didn't back down
When the rebels rode through his native town;
But held his own in the fight next day,
When all his townsfolk ran away.
That was in July, sixty-three, —
The very day that General Lee,
Flower of Southern chivalry,
Baffled and beaten, backward reeled
From a stubborn Meade and a barren field.

I might tell how, but the day before,
John Burns stood at his cottage door,
Looking down the village street,
Where, in the shade of his peaceful vine,
He heard the low of his gathered kine,
And felt their breath with incense sweet;
Or, I might say, when the sunset burned
The old farm gable, he thought it turned

The milk that fell like a babbling flood
Into the milk-pail, red as blood;
Or, how he fancied the hum of bees
Were bullets buzzing among the trees.
But all such fanciful thoughts as these
Were strange to a practical man like Burns,
Who minded only his own concerns,
Troubled no more by fancies fine
Than one of his calm-eyed, long-tailed kine, —
Quite old-fashioned and matter-of-fact,
Slow to argue, but quick to act.
That was the reason, as some folk say,
He fought so well on that terrible day.

And it was terrible.   On the right
Raged for hours the heady fight,
Thundered the battery's double bass, —
Difficult music for men to face;
While on the left, — where now the graves
Undulate like the living waves
That all the day unceasing swept
Up to the pits the rebels kept, —
Round-shot ploughed the upland glades,
Sown with bullets, reaped with blades;
Shattered fences here and there,
Tossed their splinters in the air;
The very trees were stripped and bare;

JOHN BURNS OF GETTYSBURG.

The barns that once held yellow grain
Were heaped with harvests of the slain;
The cattle bellowed on the plain,
The turkeys screamed with might and main,
And brooding barn-fowl left their rest
With strange shells bursting in each nest.

Just where the tide of battle turns,
Erect and lonely, stood old John Burns.
How do you think the man was dressed?
He wore an ancient, long buff vest,
Yellow as saffron, — but his best;
And buttoned over his manly breast
Was a bright blue coat with a rolling collar,
And large gilt buttons, — size of a dollar, —
With tails that the country-folk called " swaller.''
He wore a broad-brimmed, bell-crowned hat,
White as the locks on which it sat.
Never had such a sight been seen
For forty years on the village green,
Since old John Burns was a country beau,
And went to the " quiltings " long ago.

Close at his elbows all that day,
Veterans of the Peninsula,
Sunburnt and bearded, charged away;
And striplings, downy of lip and chin, —
Clerks that the Home-guard mustered in, —

Glanced, as they passed, at the hat he wore,
Then at the rifle his right hand bore;
And hailed him, from out their youthful lore,
With scraps of a slangy repertoire:
"How are you, White Hat?" "Put her through!"
"Your head's level!" and "Bully for you!"
Called him "Daddy,"—begged he'd disclose
The name of the tailor who made his clothes,
And what was the value he set on those;
While Burns, unmindful of jeer and scoff,
Stood there picking the rebels off,—
With his long brown rifle, and bell-crowned hat,
And the swallow-tails they were laughing at.

'Twas but a moment, for that respect
Which clothes all courage their voices checked;
And something the wildest could understand
Spake in the old man's strong right hand,
And his corded throat, and the lurking frown
Of his eyebrows under his old bell-crown;
Until, as they gazed, there crept an awe
Through the ranks in whispers, and some men saw,
In the antique vestments and long white hair,
The Past of the Nation in battle there;
And some of the soldiers since declare
That the gleam of his old white hat afar,
Like the crested plume of the brave Navarre,

JOHN BURNS OF GETTYSBURG.

That day was their oriflamme of war.
Thus raged the battle. You know the rest;
How the rebels, beaten, and backward pressed,
Broke at the final charge and ran.
At which John Burns, — a practical man, —
Shouldered his rifle, unbent his brows,
And then went back to his bees and cows.

That is the story of old John Burns;
This is the moral the reader learns:
In fighting the battle, the question's whether
You'll show a hat that's white, or a feather.

— Bret Harte.

The Picket Guard.

" ALL quiet along the Potomac," they say,
    " Except now and then a stray picket
Is shot, as he walks on his beat, to and fro,
    By a rifleman hid in the thicket.
'Tis nothing, — a private or two, now and then,
    Will not count in the news of the battle ;
Not an officer lost, — only one of the men
    Moaning out, all alone, the death-rattle."

All quiet along the Potomac to-night,
    Where the soldiers lie peacefully dreaming ;
Their tents, in the rays of the clear autumn moon,
    Or the light of the watch-fires, are gleaming.
A tremulous sigh, as the gentle night wind
    Through the forest leaves softly is creeping ;
While stars up above, with their glittering eyes,
    Keep guard, — for the army is sleeping.

There's only the sound of the lone sentry's tread,
    As he tramps from the rock to the fountain,
And thinks of the two in the low trundle-bed
    Far away in the cot on the mountain.
His musket falls slack, — his face, dark and grim,
    Grows gentle with memories tender,

THE PICKET GUARD.

As he mutters a prayer for the children asleep, —
　For their mother, — may Heaven defend her!

The moon seems to shine just as brightly as then,
　That night, when the love yet unspoken
Leaped up to his lips, — when low-murmured vows
　Were pledged to be ever unbroken.
Then drawing his sleeve roughly over his eyes,
　He dashes off tears that are welling,
And gathers his gun closer up to its place
　As if to keep down the heart-swelling.

He passes the fountain, the blasted pine-tree, —
　The footstep is lagging and weary;
Yet onward he goes, through the broad belt of light,
　Towards the shades of the forest so dreary.
Hark! was it the night wind that rustled the leaves?
　Was it the moonlight so wondrously flashing?
It looks like a rifle — ah! — " Mary, good-by! "
　And the life-blood is ebbing and plashing.

All quiet along the Potomac to-night,
　No sound save the rush of the river;
While soft falls the dew on the face of the dead, —
　The picket's off duty forever.
—Ethel Lynn Beers.

Kearney at Seven Pines.

So that soldierly legend is still on its journey, —
 That story of Kearney who knew not to yield !
'Twas the day when with Jameson, fierce Berry, and
  Birney,
 Against twenty thousand he rallied the field.
Where the red volleys poured, where the clamor rose
  highest,
 Where the dead lay in clumps through the dwarf
  oak and pine,
Where the aim from the thicket was surest and
  nighest,
 No charge like Phil Kearney's along the whole
  line.

When the battle went ill, and the bravest were
  solemn,
 Near the dark Seven Pines, where we still held
  our ground,
He rode down the length of the withering column,
 And his heart at our war-cry leapt up with a
  bound.
He snuffed, like his charger, the wind of the powder, —

His sword waved us on, and we answered the
    sign;
Loud our cheer as we rushed, but his laugh rang the
    louder;
    " There's the devil's own fun, boys, along the
      whole line ! "

How he strode his brown steed ! How we saw his
    blade brighten
    In the one hand still left, — and the reins in his
      teeth !
He laughed like a boy when the holidays heighten,
    But a soldier's glance shot from his visor beneath.
Up came the reserves to the mellay infernal,
    Asking where to go in, — through the clearing or
      pine ?
" Oh, anywhere ! Forward ! 'Tis all the same,
    colonel :
    You'll find lovely fighting along the whole line ! "

Oh, evil the black shroud of night at Chantilly,
    That hid him from sight of his brave men and
      tried !
Foul, foul sped the bullet that clipped the white lily,
    The flower of our knighthood, the whole army's
      pride !

Yet we dream that he still, — in that shadowy region
Where the dead form their ranks at the wan drum-
mer's sign, —
Rides on, as of old, down the length of his legion,
And the word still is Forward! along the whole
line.

— Edmund Clarence Stedman.

After All.

THE apples are ripe in the orchard,
  The work of the reaper is done,
And the golden woodlands redden
  In the blood of the dying sun.

At the cottage door the grandsire
  Sits pale in his easy chair,
While the gentle wind of twilight
  Plays with his silver hair.

A woman is kneeling beside him;
  A fair young head is pressed,
In the first wild passion of sorrow,
  Against his agèd breast.

And far from over the distance
  The faltering echoes come
Of the flying blast of trumpet
  And the rattling roll of the drum.

And the grandsire speaks in a whisper:
  "The end, no man can see;
But we gave him to his country,
  And we give our prayers to thee."

The violets star the meadows,
  The rosebuds fringe the door,
And over the grassy orchard
  The pink-white blossoms pour.

But the grandsire's chair is empty,
  The cottage is dark and still;
There's a nameless grave in the battle-
      field,
  And a new one under the hill.

And a pallid, tearless woman
  By the cold hearth sits alone,
And the old clock in the corner
  Ticks on with a steady drone.
                    — *William Winter.*

Sheridan's Ride.

UP from the south, at break of day,
　Bringing to Winchester fresh dismay,
The affrighted air with a shudder bore,
Like a herald in haste to the chieftain's door,
The terrible grumble, and rumble, and roar,
Telling the battle was on once more,
　And Sheridan twenty miles away.

And wider still those billows of war
Thunder'd along the horizon's bar;
And louder yet into Winchester roll'd
The roar of that red sea uncontroll'd,
Making the blood of the listener cold,
As he thought of the stake in that fiery fray,
　With Sheridan twenty miles away.

But there is a road from Winchester town,
A good broad highway leading down:
And there, through the flush of the morning light,
A steed as black as the steeds of night
Was seen to pass, as with eagle flight,
As if he knew the terrible need,
He stretch'd away with his utmost speed;

Hills rose and fell; but his heart was gay,
  With Sheridan fifteen miles away.

Still sprang from those swift hoofs, thundering south,
The dust like smoke from the cannon's mouth,
Or the trail of a comet, sweeping faster and faster,
Foreboding to traitors the doom of disaster.
The heart of the steed and the heart of the master
Were beating like prisoners assaulting their walls,
Impatient to be where the battle-field calls;
Every nerve of the charger was strained to full play,
  With Sheridan only ten miles away.

Under his spurning feet, the road
Like an arrowy Alpine river flow'd,
And the landscape sped away behind
Like an ocean flying before the wind;
And the steed, like a bark fed with furnace ire,
Swept on, with his wild eye full of fire.
But, lo! he is nearing his heart's desire;
He is snuffing the smoke of the roaring fray,
  With Sheridan only five miles away.

The first that the general saw were the groups
Of stragglers, and then the retreating troops;
What was done? what to do? a glance told him both.
Then striking his spurs with a terrible oath,

SHERIDAN'S RIDE.

He dash'd down the line, 'mid a storm of huzzas,
And the wave of retreat checked its course there,
  because
The sight of the master compell'd it to pause.
With foam and with dust the black charger was
  gray;
By the flash of his eye, and the red nostril's play,
He seem'd to the whole great army to say:
" I have brought you Sheridan all the way
  From Winchester down to save the day."

Hurrah! hurrah for Sheridan!
Hurrah! hurrah for horse and man!
And when their statues are placed on high,
Under the dome of the Union sky,
The American soldier's Temple of Fame,
There with the glorious general's name
Be it said, in letters both bold and bright:
  " Here is the steed that saved the day
By carrying Sheridan into the fight,
  From Winchester, — twenty miles away! "
                    — *Thomas Buchanan Read.*

Driving Home the Cows.

OUT of the clover and blue-eyed grass,
　　He turned them into the river-lane;
One after another he let them pass,
　　Then fastened the meadow bars again.

Under the willows, and over the hill,
　　He patiently followed their sober pace;
The merry whistle for once was still,
　　And something shadowed the sunny face.

Only a boy! and his father had said
　　He never could let his youngest go;
Two already were lying dead
　　Under the feet of the trampling foe.

But after the evening work was done,
　　And the frogs were loud in the meadow
　　　　swamp,
Over his shoulder he slung his gun,
　　And stealthily followed the footpath damp.

Across the clover and through the wheat,
　　With resolute heart and purpose grim,
Though cold was the dew on his hurrying feet,
　　And the blind bat's flitting startled him.

DRIVING HOME THE COWS.

Thrice since then had the lanes been white,
  And the orchards sweet with apple-bloom;
And now when the cows came back at night,
  The feeble father drove them home.

For news had come to the lonely farm
  That three were lying where two had lain;
And the old man's tremulous, palsied arm
  Could never lean on a son's again.

The summer day grew cold and late,
  He went for the cows when the work was
      done;
But down the lane, as he opened the gate,
  He saw them coming, one by one, —

Brindle, Ebony, Speckle, and Bess,
  Shaking their horns in the evening wind;
Cropping the buttercups out of the grass, —
  But who was it following close behind?

Loosely swung in the idle air
  The empty sleeve of army blue;
And worn and pale from the crisping hair
  Looked out a face that the father knew.

For the Southern prisons will sometimes yawn,
  And yield their dead unto life again;

And the day that comes with a cloudy dawn
  In golden glory at last may wane.

The great tears sprang to their meeting eyes;
  For the heart must speak when the lips are
      dumb;
And under the silent evening skies,
  Together they followed the cattle home.

—Kate Putnam Osgood.

Music in Camp.

TWO armies covered hill and plain,
　　Where Rappahannock's waters
Ran deeply crimsoned with the stain
　　Of battle's recent slaughters.

The summer clouds lay pitched like tents
　　In meads of heavenly azure ;
And each dread gun of the elements
　　Slept in its high embrasure.

The breeze so softly blew, it made
　　No forest leaf to quiver ;
And the smoke of the random cannonade
　　Rolled slowly from the river.

And now, where circling hills looked down
　　With cannon grimly planted,
O'er listless camp and silent town
　　The golden sunset slanted.

When on the fervid air there came
　　A strain, now rich, now tender,
The music seemed itself aflame
　　With day's departing splendor.

A Federal band, which eve and morn
  Played measures brave and nimble,
Had just struck up, with flute and horn
  And lively clash of cymbal.

Down flocked the soldiers to the banks;
  Till, margined by its pebbles,
One wooded shore was blue with "Yanks,"
  And one was gray with "Rebels."

Then all was still; and then the band,
  With movement light and tricksy,
Made stream and forest, hill and strand,
  Reverberate with "Dixie."

The conscious stream, with burnished glow,
  Went proudly o'er its pebbles,
But thrilled throughout its deepest flow
  With yelling of the Rebels.

Again a pause; and then again
  The trumpet pealed, sonorous,
And "Yankee Doodle" was the strain
  To which the shore gave chorus.

The laughing ripple shoreward flew
  To kiss the shining pebbles;
Loud shrieked the swarming Boys in Blue
  Defiance to the Rebels.

MUSIC IN CAMP.

And yet once more the bugle sang
  Above the stormy riot;
No shout upon the evening rang,—
  There reigned a holy quiet.

The sad, slow stream its noiseless flood
  Poured o'er the glistening pebbles;
All silent now the Yankees stood,
  All silent stood the Rebels.

No unresponsive soul had heard
  That plaintive note's appealing,
So deeply " Home, Sweet Home " had stirred
  The hidden founts of feeling.

Or Blue, or Gray, the soldier sees,
  As by the wand of fairy,
The cottage 'neath the live oak trees,
  The cabin by the prairie.

Or cold, or warm, his native skies
  Bend in their beauty o'er him;
Seen through the tear-mist in his eyes,
  His loved ones stand before him.

As fades the iris after rain
  In April's tearful weather,
The vision vanished as the strain
  And daylight died together.

But Memory, waked by Music's art,
   Expressed in simple numbers,
Subdued the sternest Yankee's heart,
   Made light the Rebel's slumbers.

And fair the form of Music shines, —
   That bright celestial creature, —
Who still 'mid War's embattled lines
   Gave this one touch of Nature.

          —John R. Thompson.

Three Hundred Thousand More.

WE are coming, Father Abraham, three hundred
    thousand more,
From Mississippi's winding stream and from New
    England's shore;
We leave our ploughs and workshops, our wives and
    children dear,
With hearts too full for utterance, with but a silent
    tear;
We dare not look behind us, but steadfastly before:
We are coming, Father Abraham, three hundred
    thousand more!

If you look across the hilltops that meet the northern
    sky,
Long moving lines of rising dust your vision may
    descry;
And now the wind, an instant, tears the cloudy veil
    aside,
And floats aloft our spangled flag in glory and in
    pride,
And bayonets in the sunlight gleam, and bands brave
    music pour:
We are coming, Father Abraham, three hundred
    thousand more!

If you look all up our valleys where the growing harvests shine,
You may see our sturdy farmer boys fast forming into
line;
And children from their mothers' knees are pulling at
the weeds,
And learning how to reap and sow against their country's needs;
And a farewell group stands weeping at every cottage
door;
We are coming, Father Abraham, three hundred
thousand more!

You have called us, and we're coming, by Richmond's
bloody tide
To lay us down, for Freedom's sake, our brothers'
bones beside,
Or from foul treason's savage grasp to wrench the
murderous blade,
And in the face of foreign foes its fragments to
parade.
Six hundred thousand loyal men and true have gone
before:
We are coming, Father Abraham, three hundred
thousand more!

Cavalry Song.

OUR good steeds snuff the evening air,
 Our pulses with their purpose tingle;
The foeman's fires are twinkling there;
 He leaps to hear our sabres jingle!
  Halt!
Each carbine sends its whizzing ball:
Now, cling! clang! forward all,
  Into the fight!

Dash on beneath the smoking dome:
 Through level lightnings gallop nearer!
One look to Heaven! No thoughts of home:
 The guidons that we bear are dearer.
  Charge!
Cling! clang! forward all!
Heaven help those whose horses fall!
  Cut left and right!

They flee before our fierce attack!
 They fall! they spread in broken surges!
Now, comrades, bear our wounded back,
 And leave the foeman to his dirges.
  Wheel!

The bugles sound the swift recall:
Cling! clang! backward all!
    Home, and good night!
        — *Edmund Clarence Stedman.*

Marching Still.

SHE is old, and bent, and wrinkled,
　　In her rocker in the sun,
And the thick, gray, woollen stocking
　　That she knits is never done.
She will ask the news of battle
　　If you pass her when you will,
For to her the troops are marching,
　　　　Marching still.

Seven tall sons about her growing
　　Cheered the widowed mother's soul;
One by one they kissed and left her
　　When the drums began to roll.
They are buried in the trenches,
　　They are bleaching on the hill;
But to her the boys are marching,
　　　　Marching still.

She was knitting in the corner
　　When the fatal news was read,
How the last and youngest perished, —
　　And the letter, ending, said:
" I am writing on my knapsack
　　By the road, with borrowed quill,

For the Union army's marching,
    Marching still."

Reason sank and died within her
    Like a flame for want of air;
So she knits the woollen stockings
    For the soldier lads to wear,
Waiting till the war is ended
    For her sons to cross the sill;
For she thinks they all are marching,
    Marching still.
                — *Minna Irving.*

The Battle-cry of Freedom.

YES, we'll rally 'round the flag, boys, we'll rally
once again,
Shouting the battle-cry of freedom,
We will rally from the hillside, we'll gather from the
plain,
Shouting the battle-cry of freedom.

CHORUS.

The Union forever, hurrah, boys, hurrah,
Down with the traitor, up with the star,
While we rally 'round the flag, boys, rally once again,
Shouting the battle-cry of freedom.

We are springing to the call of our brothers gone be-
fore,
Shouting the battle-cry of freedom,
And we'll fill the vacant ranks with a million freemen
more,
Shouting the battle-cry of freedom. — Cho.

We will welcome to our numbers the loyal, true, and
brave,
Shouting the battle-cry of freedom,

And altho' they may be poor, not a man shall be a
    slave,
  Shouting the battle-cry of freedom. — CHO.

So we're springing to the call from the East and
    from the West,
  Shouting the battle-cry of freedom,
And we'll hurl the rebel crew from the land we love
    the best,
  Shouting the battle-cry of freedom. — CHO.

The Cavalry Charge.

HARK! the rattling roar of the musketeers,
   And the ruffled drums, and the rallying cheers,
And the rifles burn with a keen desire
Like the crackling whips of a hemlock fire,
And the singing shot, and the shrieking shell,
And the splintered fire on the shattered hell,
And the great white breaths of the cannon smoke
As the growling guns by batteries spoke;
And the ragged gaps in the walls of blue
Where the iron surge rolled heavily through,
That the colonel builds with a breath again
As he cleaves the din with his " *Close up, men!* "
And the groan torn out from the blackened lips,
And the prayer doled slow with the crimsoned drips,
And the beaming look in the dying eye
As under the cloud the stars go by,
" *But his soul marched on!* " the captain said,
For the Boy in Blue can never be dead!
And the troopers sit in their saddles all
Like statues carved in an ancient hall,
And they watch the whirl from their breathless
      ranks,
And their spurs are close to the horses' flanks,

And the fingers work of the sabre hand, —
Oh, to bid them live; and to make them grand!
And the bugle sounds to the charge at last,
And away they plunge, and the front is passed!
And the jackets blue grow red as they ride,
And the scabbards, too, that clank by their side,
And the dead soldiers deaden the strokes iron-shod
As they gallop right on o'er the plashy red sod, —
Right into the cloud all spectral and dim,
Right up to the guns black-throated and grim,
Right down on the hedges bordered with steel,
Right through the dense columns, — then, "*Right
      about wheel!*"
Hurrah! a new swath through the harvest again!
Hurrah for the Flag!   To the battle, Amen!

— Benjamin F. Taylor.

The Black Regiment.

DARK as the clouds of even,
  Ranked in the western heaven,
Waiting the breath that lifts
All the dead mass, and drifts
Tempest and falling brand
Over a ruined land, —
So still and orderly,
Arm to arm, knee to knee,
Waiting the great event,
Stands the black regiment.

Down the long dusky line
Teeth gleam, and eyeballs shine ;
And the bright bayonet,
Bristling and firmly set,
Flashed with a purpose grand,
Long ere the sharp command
Of the fierce rolling drum
Told them their time had come,
Told them what work was sent
For the black regiment.

" Now," the flag-sergeant cried,
" Though death and hell betide,
Let the whole nation see
If we are fit to be
Free in this land; or bound
Down, like the whining hound, —
Bound with red stripes of pain
In our cold chains again ! "
Oh, what a shout there went
From the black regiment !

" Charge ! " trump and drum awoke;
Onward the bondsmen broke;
Bayonet and sabre-stroke
Vainly opposed their rush.
Through the wild battle's crush,
With but one thought aflush,
Driving their lords like chaff,
In the gun's mouth they laugh;
Or at the slippery brands,
Leaping with open hands,
Down they tear man and horse,
Down in their awful course;
Trampling with bloody heel
Over the crushing steel, —
All their eyes forward bent,
Rushed the black regiment.

" Freedom ! " their battle-cry, —
" Freedom ! or leave to die ! "
Ah ! and they meant the word,
Not as with us 'tis heard, —
Not a mere party shout ;
They gave their spirits out,
Trusted the end to God,
And on the gory sod
Rolled in triumphant blood.
Glad to strike one free blow,
Whether for weal or woe ;
Glad to breathe one free breath,
Though on the lips of death ;
Praying — alas ! in vain ! —
That they might fall again,
So they could once more see
That burst to liberty !
This was what " freedom " lent
To the black regiment.

Hundreds on hundreds fell ;
But they are resting well ;
Scourges, and shackles strong,
Never shall do them wrong.
Oh, to the living few,
Soldiers, be just and true !

Hail them as comrades tried;
Fight with them side by side.
Never, in field or tent,
Scorn the black regiment!

     — George H. Boker.

THE WAR WITH SPAIN

On the Eve of War.

O GOD of Battles, who art still
    The God of Love, the God of Rest,
Subdue thy people's fiery will,
    And quell the passions in their breast!
Before we bathe our hands in blood
We lift them to thy Holy Rood.

The waiting nations hold their breath
    To catch the dreadful battle-cry;
And in the silence as of death
    The fateful hours go softly by.
Oh, hear thy people where they pray,
And shrive our souls before the fray!

Before the sun of peace shall set,
    We kneel apart a solemn while;
Pity the eyes with sorrow wet,
    But pity most the lips that smile.
The night comes fast; we hear afar
The baying of the wolves of war.

Not lightly, oh, not lightly, Lord,
    Let this our awful task begin;

Speak from thy throne a warning word
  Above the angry factions' din.
If *this* be thy Most Holy will,
Be with us still, — be with us still!

                    — Danske Dandridge.

Good Friday, 1898.

Answering to Roll-call.

THIS one fought with Jackson, and faced the fight
    with Lee;
That one followed Sherman as he galloped to the
    sea;
But they're marchin' on together just as friendly as
    can be,
And they'll answer to the roll-call in the mornin'!

    They'll rally to the fight,
    In the stormy day and night,
In bonds that no cruel fate shall sever;
    While the storm-winds waft on high
    Their ringing battle-cry:
" Our country, — our country forever!"

The brave old flag above them is rippling down its
    red, —
Each crimson stripe the emblem of the blood by
    heroes shed;
It shall wave for them victorious or droop above
    them, — dead,
For they'll answer to the roll-call in the mornin'!

They'll rally to the fight
In the stormy day and night,
In bonds that no cruel fate shall sever;
While their far-famed battle-cry
Shall go ringing to the sky:
" Our country, — our country forever ! "

— *Frank L. Stanton.*

New Beacons Set.

To the heroes of the war-ship *Maine*.

NO more, no more shall come the brave —
　　The champions of the free —
Who bore our flag upon the wave
　　From farthest sea to sea.

No cheer shall rise from sailor lip
　　To greet the starry fold,
The ensign of the gallant ship
　　Shall be no more unroll'd!

Three hundred heroes in their might
　　Their country's summons heard —
Thrice-sworn to guard their country's right
　　From harm of deed or word;

Nor trustier band e'er faced a foe
　　Upon the surging deep,
Nor met the thousand-shotted blow
　　Along the bloody steep!

Not theirs the fierce delight to feel
　　The fury of the fray, —
To know their steel quick answered steel
　　Where foemen barr'd the way;

But in the shadow of the gloom
   That 'round the proud ship fell,
There burst the awful roar of doom
   And fires of sudden hell!

They died as only men can die
   Who follow, as their star,
Grim Duty's light — nor question why —
   Thro' paths of peace and war!

Beside the sea their graves are set, —
   Beneath the surging foam, —
And many a Northland eye is wet
   Because they come not home!

They come not home forevermore,
   But evermore they'll be,
From lake to gulf, from shore to shore,
   New beacons to the free, —

New lights upon the rocky coasts
   To guide our Ship of State;
New proof how hearts, too brave for boasts,
   In serving may be great!

                    —John Jerome Rooney.

"Remember the Maine."

WHEN the vengeance wakes, when the battle
    breaks,
  And the ships sweep out to sea,
When the foe is neared and the decks are cleared
  And the colors floating free,
When the squadrons meet, when it's fleet to fleet
  And front to front with Spain,
From ship to ship, from lip to lip,
    Pass on the quick refrain,
    "Remember, remember the *Maine !*"

When the flag shall sign, "Advance in line;
  Train ships on an even keel,"
When the guns shall flash and the shot shall crash
  And bound on the ringing steel,
When the rattling blasts from the armored masts
  Are hurling their deadliest rain,
Let their voices loud, through the blinding cloud,
  Cry ever the fierce refrain,
    "Remember, remember the *Maine !*"

God's sky and sea in that storm shall be
  Fate's chaos of smoke and flame,

But across that hell every shot shall tell,
  Not a gun can miss its aim;
Not a blow shall fail on the crumbling mail,
  And the waves that engulf the slain
Shall sweep the decks of the blackened wrecks
  With the thundering, dread refrain,
  " Remember, remember the *Maine !* "

— *Robert Burns Wilson.*

The Maine's Men.

DEATH came out of the black night's deep,
  And steered for a battle-ship's side;
But never a man of the sailor clan
  Looked on the Deathman's ride.

The Kansas lad and the Hampshire boy,
  And the boy from Tennessee,
With never a fear that death was near,
  Swung into eternity.

Nor flag, nor shot, nor battle-cry,
  Nor strain of the Nation's air,
Broke into the gloom of the sailor's doom,
  Nor yet a priestly prayer.

There looks a face from a far-away home,
  With eye bent on the sea,
For the Hampshire Jack who'll ne'er come back,
  Nor the lad from Tennessee.

Not theirs was the glory of battle
  No victory crowned the day,
But a Nation weeps that the dark sea keeps
  Her dead beneath the bay.

                    — Mexico Two Republics.

Song of the Rapid-fires.

YOU may take the thirteen-inchers,
    And the eights and six and fours;
You may take the heavy battery,
    And the rain of shells it pours;
You may take the grim projectile
    And the mighty solid shot,
But we, the rapid-firers,
    Are the guns that make things hot.
        Oh, it's swift the turrets swing us,
            And with steady, ready ken
        We reach the decks and sweep them
            With their living walls of men!
        It's ping, and sping, and splutter,
            And it's beautiful to be
        The tenors in the chorus
            That is sung across the sea!

Swing your broadside into action,
    Let the forward turrets play,
Hark the thunder of the cannon
    As they dance in death's chassé!
Sweep the courses with the squadron,
    Let them give and take again,

SONG OF THE RAPID-FIRES.

Send the foe the thunder-challenge, —
  But it's we that take the men!
    Oh, it's terrible to hear us,
      And it's lively when we sing,
    As across the heaving billows
      To the foemen's deck we spring;
  We are tenors of the chorus,
    But on starboard or on lee
  We are heard above the thunder
    That is sung across the sea!

We are flame and fire and terror,
  We are twenty to their one;
We are up again and at them
  Ere they charge the heavy gun;
And our lips are red with battle,
  And our throats are hoarse with smoke,
When we land upon their quarter
  And they feel our lightning stroke.
    Oh, it's rapid, rapid, rapid,
      Jolly rapid-fires are we,
    Singing 'round the ranging turret
      And across the surging sea.
    We are brothers to the heavies
      And we strike where they have missed,
    And there's doom upon the quarter
      Where our twenty bolts have kissed.

Swing the pounders into action,
  We shall beat the batteries yet!
From the furnace to the funnel,
  Where the naked seamen sweat,
We are heard amid the chorus,
  And they know our surging shout,
As we sing across the waters
  From our triple-steel redoubt.
    Oh, it's rip and roar and rumble
      When the thirteens sink the foe,
    And it's death upon the billows
      When the solid pounders go;
    But it's swift the turrets swing us
      And with steady, ready ken
    We search the decks and sweep them
      With their living walls of men!

                    —*Baltimore News.*

To Spain — A Last Word.

IBERIAN! palter no more! By thine hands,
    thine alone, they were slain!
  Oh, 'twas a deed in the dark —
              Yet mark!
We will show you a way — only one — by which ye
    may blot out the stain!

Build them a monument whom to death-sleep, in
    their sleep, ye betrayed!
  Proud and stern let it be —
              Cuba free!
So, only, the stain shall be razed — so, only, the great
    debt be paid!

                    — *Edith M. Thomas.*

Cuba.

Originally published in 1858.

O'ER thy purple hills, O Cuba!
  Through thy valleys of romance,
All thy glorious dreams of freedom
  Are but dreamt as in a trance.

Mountain pass and fruitful valley,
  Mural town and spreading plain,
Show the footsteps of the Spaniard,
  In his burning lust for gain.

Since the caravel of Colon
  Grated first upon thy strand,
Ev'rything about thee, Cuba,
  Shows the iron Spanish hand.

Hear that crash of martial music?
  From the plaza how it swells!
How it trembles with the meaning
  Of the story that it tells!

Turn thy steps up to Artares, —
  There was done a deed of shame!
Helpless men were coldly butchered, —
  'Tis a part of Spanish fame.

CUBA.

Wander now down to the Punta, —
  Lay thy hand upon thy throat, —
Thou wilt see a Spanish emblem
  In the dark and grim garrote.

In the Moro, — in the Market, —
  In the shadow, — in the sun, —
Thou wilt see the bearded Spaniard,
  Where a gold piece may be won.

And they fatten on thee, Cuba!
  Gay Soldado, — cunning priest, —
How these vultures flock and hover,
  On thy tortured breast to feast!

Thou Prometheus of the ocean,
  Bound down, — not for what thou'st done,
But for fear thy social statue
  Should start living in the sun!

And we give thee tears, O Cuba!
  And our prayers to God uplift,
That at last the flame celestial
  May come down to thee, — a gift!
                              —*J. B. Hope.*

Cuba.

SHE is fighting for her freedom, striving hard to
    rend in twain
The base chains that hold her captive at the feet of
    cruel Spain,
While the iron hand of power, stretching out across
    the sea,
Seeks to crush the infant nation in her struggle to be
    free.

Like fierce wolves the armored war-ships flock about
    her naked coasts,
And her verdant fields are trampled by the feet of
    hostile hosts.
Grim Destruction's form stalks onward in the battle-
    blighted path,
Smiting all her land with terror in his dire, unsparing
    wrath.

There is not an arm to shield her, and no helping
    hand is found,
That will aid to break the fetters that so long have
    held her bound.

CUBA.

All the nations gaze with coldness at her travail and
    her woe,
Leaving her alone to grapple with her stern, relentless
    foe.

She may fail, — sink overpower'd by the fierce in-
    vading bands,
And her good lance fall in splinters from her firm,
    unflinching hands,
For the battle is not always with the ones whose
    cause is just,
And the tyrant's sword has sometimes laid fair Free-
    dom in the dust.

She may sink, like poor, lost Poland, vanquished in a
    righteous fray,
And Oppression's cruel vultures flock about their
    helpless prey ;
But the kindly hearts of millions, loving liberty and
    right,
Beat for her in her brave struggle, in her thraldom,
    and her night.

                         —James Gardner.

Cuba, 1897.

O GOD! that I might breathe of Freedom's air;
   Alone I weep to-day, alone, forlorn, —
Twin sister of pale Sorrow, wan and worn;
Low, low I kneel with dark dishevelled hair.

My noblest, bravest sons lie starving where
   Grim Morro looms on high; my flesh is torn
   And bleeding from the tyrant's lash; I mourn
My children slain; I cry in my despair

For some protecting arm, — some flashing sword
   Upraised in my defence; I cry, and yet
      All lands stand dumb and will not answer me.
How long ere my deep prayer be heard, O Lord,
   How long ere my bruised feet be firmly set
      Upon the radiant peak of Liberty?

— Herbert Bashford.

Cußa, 1898.

LAND of languor and of beauty, where the tawny
sunset blending
In a blaze of gold and scarlet from the hillside to
the sea, —
Where the rose-scent softly lingers and the drowsy
palms are bending
In a reverent obeisance ere the day shall cease to
be;

Land of music and of moonlight, where the gorgeous
flowers are gleaming
In chaotic chords of color in the palace gardens
fair,
And the fountains sing and tinkle in the wonder of
your dreaming,
And the birds of brilliant plumage flash and flame
upon the air;

Land of legend and of story, with your sultriness and
splendor,
And your skies of purest sapphire so ethereally
blue;
All the universe has wakened to a vast compassion
tender,

And the sons of men stand breathless, for the world
    is watching you.

In the majesty of morning, when the sunshine spreads
    and glistens
    In a myriad shining spangles on the forest and the
        sward,
Rings the war-cry of your legions; and the poltroon
    Spaniard listens,
    And he trembles in an ague at the slogan of the
        sword.

In the marshes and morasses, where the cobra coils
    and hisses,
    And your heroes who have fallen in the fight
        serenely lie;
All their sleeping is the sweeter for the tender
    breeze's kisses, —
    And the buzzard sails and circles like a sentinel on
        high.

Cuba ! — Paradise of beauty ! — Hell of tyrant's cold
    devising ! —
    Made a shambles and a charnel-house thro' twice
        a hundred years !
I can hear the utter anguish of a million mothers
    rising

CUBA, 1898.

In a wilderness of weeping, — in a hurricane of
    tears!

Stand to arms, you men of valor! For the conflict's
    almost over,
    And the waking world stands panting to acclaim a
        people free;
For the fetters fall and crumble, and the Spaniard
    skulks to cover,
    As the bells clang out a tocsin from the mountains
        to the sea.

And your land shall live in loveliness! The hillside
    and the river
    And the flowers that bloom and bourgeon shall pro-
        claim the glad release;
And your name shall stand untarnished on the Scroll
    of Fame forever;
    You have fought and bled for glory, — you shall
        know the bliss of peace.

— Harold R. Vyne.

The Gathering.

WE are coming, Cuba, — coming; our starry
banner shines
Above the swarming legions, sweeping downward
to the sea.
From Northern hill, and Western plain, and towering Southern pines
The serried hosts are gathering, — and Cuba shall
be free.

We are coming, Cuba, — coming. Thy sturdy patriots brave,
Who fight as fought our fathers in the old time
long ago,
Shall see the Spanish squadrons sink beneath the
whelming wave,
And plant their own loved banner on the ramparts
of their foe.

We are coming, Cuba, — coming. Across the billow's foam
Our gallant ships are bearing our bravest down to
thee,

THE GATHERING.

While earnest prayers are rising from every free-
    man's home
That freedom's God may lead them on, and Cuba
    shall be free.

— Herbert B. Swett.

Our Boys Are Marching on.

WE heard the music ringing from the camps of
    long ago;
The solemn tramp of armies, as they marched to
    meet the foe;
We echo back their battle-song, that all the world
    may know
      Our flag is marching on!

CHORUS.

    Long ago the boys were marching;
    North and South to battle marching;
    Now together they are marching, —
      Together marching on.
    Marching on to fields of glory,
    Marching on to deeds of glory,
    Hear again the nation's story, —
      Our boys are marching on!

We heard the bugle calling to the sons of Blue and
    Gray;
Our veterans were falling, one by one, beside the
    way;
They'll join with us in singing, on their next Me-
    morial day, —
      Our boys are marching on!

OUR BOYS ARE MARCHING ON.

CHORUS.

Blue and Gray are now united;
North and South are now united;
'Round the flag with hearts united, —
    Together marching on.
Marching on to fields of glory;
Marching on to deeds of glory;
Hear again their ringing story, —
    Our boys are marching on!

We heard the voice of wailing, — Cuba writhing in
    her pain;
" Deliver us, your neighbors, from the clutch of cruel
    Spain."
We are coming, Cuba libre, to redeem you and the
    Maine, —
    Old Glory's marching on!

CHORUS.

Spain must go, and go forever;
Cuba's chains the sword must sever;
Yanks and Johnnies falter never, —
    Together marching on.
Marching on to fields of glory;
Marching on to deeds of glory;
Sing again the dear old story, —
    Of Freedom marching on!

There's a breeze from off the ocean, bringing mem-
    ories of the past ;
Of the flag that waved in triumph, — we will nail it
    to the mast !
There is glory for our Navy, and for Spain the die is
    cast, —
    Our Navy's sailing on !

CHORUS.

Sailing on, with Dewey sailing ;
Sailing on, with Sampson sailing ;
Sailing on, our Schley is sailing,
    Wherever glory's won.
Glory, glory for our Navy ;
Glory, glory for our Navy ;
Hear the echoes from our Navy ;
    Our Navy's sailing on !

            —John H. Jewett.

Battle=ship and Torpedo=Boat.

SMOOTH and lean, — they have stripped her
   clean
  Down to her leering guns.
A-weather and lee she smashes the sea
  With her weight of ten thousand tons,
From bow to stern her watchers turn
  The beams of her searching suns.

A-wash, half-drowned, we speed around
  To beat the veering light,
For she must see, ere her fangs are free,
  That she may begin to bite,
And we laugh where we lie, at the blundering eye
  That misses us in the night.

They have freighted her with five hundred men;
  She is fierce with rifled guns;
But she cannot mark, as she rolls in the dark,
  The death that comes and runs.
We flit as a mist-wreath on the sea,
  And ere her topmen leap
We have struck and fled, and the riven dead
  Are sucked in the whirling deep.

—J. W. M.

The Twins in the Turret.

FIRST RIFLE.

CAN you see her, O my brother?
　　Can you sight her through the rack?
Is that streak across the smother
　　Coal smoke trailing from a stack?
Do you hear how louder, clearer
　　Sounds the throbbing of our screws?
When we come a little nearer,
　　Which of us shall hail her?　Choose!

SECOND RIFLE.

Let me send a brief opinion
　　Of the murders on the *Maine;*
Of the Eagle's new dominion,
　　When we've closed accounts with Spain, —
There, they've passed the word to crowd her,
　　Here's our squad, too, on the run.
Glad we've got this smokeless powder.
　　Now, look out, — you'll see the fun.

FIRST RIFLE.

Are you ready, brother, ready
　　With your thunderbolt of steel?

THE TWINS IN THE TURRET.

Have they got your bearings steady?
  Gods, you made the whole world reel!
Now it's my turn; what, you hit her
  In her vitals?   Oh, what bliss!
There is naught in life as bitter
  For a rifle as a miss.

SECOND RIFLE.

All hell's loose; there's no use talking.
  That's the time you ripped her wide!
Look, there's Davy Jones a-walking,
  Picking Spaniards from the tide.
Hi! But it's a howling racket,
  For a great, long, silent gun!
Easy, now, don't burst your jacket!
  Our death-dealing work is done.

—John Paul Bocock.

A Hymn of Our Armies.

I HEAR the sound at midnight of the tramp of
many feet;
It rolls from country highways, it echoes from the
street;
I hear its murmurs meet, and swell, and surge like
waters fleet,
  Marching, marching, marching, marching, marching on!

I listen in the daybreak to the noise of rolling cars,
With their freight of living valor sweeping south-
ward to the wars;
From every commonwealth beneath our country's
flashing stars,
  Rolling, rolling, rolling, rolling, rolling on!

Through the morning comes a wailing up from over
all the land,
Mothers weeping for their sons who pass among the
moving band,
Wives mourning for the husbands they have lent
with loyal hand
  To their country's risen legions marching on.

A HYMN OF OUR ARMIES.

There are flashes — not of sunrise — from the islands
    far a-sea,
Where the mists are shot with lightnings of the hot
    artillery,
And the cloud of battle brightens with the sun of
    victory,
  In the eyes of many nations shining on.

And my spirit hears an answer from the islands of
    the south,
Where the nation's heart is speaking through the
    cannon's smoky mouth;
'Tis the voice of burdened peoples, from amid their
    pain and drouth,
  Shouting glory to the mighty marching on!

And while I watch and listen, my soul within is
    stirred,
And I catch a gladder message than mine ears to-day
    have heard,
'Tis the spirit of my country with her everlasting
    word
  Chanting freedom to all people drawing on.

As it was from the beginning, to the end that word
    shall be

God's light to peoples captive, God's life to peoples
    free.
Speaking nearer, clearer, dearer, its sweet creed of
    liberty,
To the heights of noblest glory rolling on !

— O. C. Auringer.

For Cuba.

NO precedent, ye say, '
　　To point the glorious way
Towards help for one downtrod in blood and tears?
　　Brothers, 'tis time there were !
　　We bare our swords for her,
And set a model for the coming years!

　　This act, to end her pain,
　　Without a hope of gain, '
Its like on history's page where can ye read?
　　Humanity and God
　　Call us to paths untrod !
On, brothers, on! we follow not, but lead!

—Robert Mowry Bell.

Under the Stars and Stripes.

HIGH on the world did our fathers of old,
 Under the stars and stripes,
Blazon the name that we now must uphold,
 Under the stars and stripes.
Vast in the past they have builded an arch
Over which freedom has lighted her torch.
Follow it! Follow it! Come, let us march
 Under the stars and stripes!

We in whose bodies the blood of them runs,
 Under the stars and stripes,
We will acquit us as sons of their sons,
 Under the stars and stripes,
Ever for justice, our heel upon wrong,
We in the light of our vengeance thrice strong!
Rally together! Come tramping along
 Under the stars and stripes!

Out of our strength and a nation's great need,
 Under the stars and stripes,
Heroes again as of old we shall breed,
 Under the stars and stripes.

UNDER THE STARS AND STRIPES.

Broad to the winds be our banner unfurled !
Straight in Spain's face let defiance be hurled !
God on our side, we will battle the world
    Under the stars and stripes !

              — *Madison Cawein.*

The Song of Manila.

AS it began to dawn, you know,
   Just at the peep of day,
Ere yet the sun was fully up
   Above Manila Bay, —

We crept into their port, my boy,
   Their crews were sound asleep;
Crept close upon their forts and ships,
   Glassed in the quiet deep.

But when the Spanish sluggards woke,
   Upspringing with the sun,
They sent across the shining wave
   A booming, harmless gun.

No answer first, — we but swept on;
   Then lo! a flash of flame,
A sound of thunder, — ha, my boy,
   And thus began our game!

How roared the cannon, sang the bombs,
   And whistled shell and shot;
How crashed their splintered masts and spars
   As all the air grew hot!

THE SONG OF MANILA.

How worked our tars, — a hero each, —
 Their sooty breasts swelled high,
Remembering that on us was fixed
 Our country's grateful eye!

And that while through black clouds of smoke
 The sun gleamed fiery red,
There flew, with every star undimmed,
 Old Glory overhead!

And through it all God's hand, my boy,
 In this fierce fight was plain;
Not one brave lad of ours fell dead,
 As we avenged the *Maine!*

But scores of Spanish, — and they, too,
 Had done their duty well, —
May God have mercy on their souls,
 Be they in heaven or hell!

Their ships we captured, sunk or burned,
 And live a thousand years,
I'll thank the Lord I, too, was there, —
 Hear still our ringing cheers!

Hail to our noble Commodore,
 For deeds so glorious done,
Praise to a greater Captain still,
 For such a victory won.

As echoing through all time, will tell
  About Manila Bay,
What manhood dared, how freedom fought,
  On that immortal day!
                    — *Stuart Sterne.*

The Red and the Blue.

OH, Johnny Bull! you know, John,
   "Since we have been acquaint,"
Your many little tricks would try
   The patience of a saint.
But with the world against you
   A sturdy front you show;
I guess we'll have to back you,
   And let old bygones go!

You've proved a valiant foe, John,
   In many a bloody fight;
So now we'll stand together,
   And strike for truth and right.
And should the foreign beagles
   Bay the lion in his lair,
You'll find the Yankee eagle's
   Beak and talons will be bare!

What though our name be changed, John,
   It has not changed the breed,
Both stately trees have sprung from
   The Anglo-Saxon seed.
Both nations' rights are equal,
   Wrung from a monarch's greed,

Our Seventy-six the sequel
  Of glorious Runnymede!

Grip hands across the ocean,
  And should there come a time, —
When needed, — I've a notion
  You'll see the "thin red line."
With shoulder pressed to shoulder,
  Stanch friends and comrades true,
Old England's scarlet Tommies,
  And our bold boys in blue.

Fling out the red cross banner!
  Too long has it been furled.
We'll plant "Old Glory" by its side
  And then defy the world!
Woe to the foreign foemen
  Who front the battle-line,
Where Johnny's cross and Sammy's stars
  Their colors bright entwine!

— H. A. Roby.

The New Toreador.

BRAVO, Jonathan! Now's your time, —
  We're getting tired of brag and bluster,
Make a bid for the true sublime, —
  Add to honor the final lustre.
Banderillos were very well,
  Waving scarfs and avoiding dances;
Now comes the struggle, — who can tell
  Upon which side are the better chances?

Wait till the ring begins to hum,
  Ramping and snorting, stamping, raging,
With blare of trumpets and roll of drums,
  But doesn't quite know whom he's engaging.
Wait there, Jonathan, calm and cool;
  More than your match some people think him.
Never mind that, — keep cool, and you'll
  Remain unhurt while you deftly pink him.

Steady, Jonathan! All mankind
  Gazes at you in silent wonder.
Most, to your virtues deaf and blind,
  Think your attitude's just a blunder.
Britain, however, is stanch and true,
  On your side are our hearts enlisted!

Maybe, sir, 'twill occur to you
　That we might turn the tail you've often twisted.

Blood of our blood, we are all for you,
　Against whomever you make attacks on.
The racial tie, though strained, holds true.
　" Bully for you ! " cries the Anglo-Saxon.
Moral support is all you need,
　Else had we strode " the ring " together, —
Until the wide world's saved and freed,
　Bound are we in a moral tether.

Stand firm, Jonathan, let him come.
　What's the use of some little brushes ?
Wait till the ring begins to hum
　With the wildest rush of his angry rushes.
Stand firm, Jonathan !　He's at bay ;
　His wrath he never can calm or smother.
Stand you firm, for the coming fray
　Means death for one or death for the other.

One of his breed, long years ago,
　With desperate, deadly, stern insistence,
With equal wrath and greater show
　Threatened our national existence.

THE NEW TOREADOR.

Then we baited him, — drove him back, —
  The old sea-dogs rushed out to meet him ;
Taught him a lesson in attack ;
  Showed him how Englishmen meant to greet him.

Feebler son of that far-off sire, —
  Still he'll fight, for there's no retreating ;
Feebler, aye, but the self-same ire,
  Still a foe who will take some beating.
Stand firm, Jonathan, — show your pluck ;
  Sooner or later you're bound to meet him.
Face him valiantly, and, with luck
  Helping you, you will soundly beat him.

Yours the strength of the Saxon race,
  Heart of oak, in its steel nerves banded,
Death and danger you still may face,
  Open foe or the underhanded.
Quietly does it.   Wait his rush, —
  Keep your power still undiminished.
Strike, as upon you he seems to crush, —
  Strike, and the deadly fray is finished.

Bravo, Jonathan !   Now's your time.
  Gone forever the days of bluster.

Make a bid for the true sublime
  With all the power that you can muster.
Banderillos were very well,
  Waving scarfs and avoiding dances;
Now comes the struggle; skill will tell,
  Conquering weight and compelling chances.
                              — *London Fun.*

𝕭eneath the 𝕱lag.

ON the sunny hillside sleeping,
　On the calm and placid plain,
By the rivers swiftly sweeping,
　By the rudely roaring main,
Lie the men who saved the nation
　In the dark hour long ago,
Meeting death with proud elation
　From a brave but erring foe.

In their earthly sleep unending
　Do the nations martyred sons
Hear the war shouts hoarsely blending
　With the booming of the guns?
Do they quicken at the rattle
　As the mighty band sweeps by?
Do they see that still in battle
　Heroes rise to do or die?

Let us hope these warriors knighted
　In the bright hereafter know
That our nation firm united
　Faces now a common foe;

That beneath the dear Old Glory,
  Clearing freedom's splendid way,
Adding lustre to its story,
  Side by side march Blue and Gray !
                    —*Cleveland Plain Dealer.*

Patriotism at Squawville.

TIMES is mighty dull at Squawville, an' we've
　　nothin' else to do,
Fur to serve as daily pastime and to keep from gittin'
　　blue,
But to loaf around the gin-mill an' discuss the latest
　　news,
An' absorb the fiery substance known to scientists as
　　booze.
A-discussin' of the rumpus with the Spaniards, pro
　　and con,
Has become the leadin' feature; we begin the gab at
　　dawn
When we sip our mornin' bracer, an' we talk about
　　the fight
Till we go a-whoopin' homeward quite how-come-
　　you-so at night.

There's a dif'rence of opinion as to how the powers
　　that are
Back at Washington assembled should proceed to
　　run the war;
But upon the vital question that ol' Cuba should be
　　free
As a comprehensive unit we unanimous agree.

As the news kep' gittin' hotter all our patr'otism riz,
In a figgerative manner, till you 'most could hear
it sizz,
An' at frequent intermissions while a chawin' of the
rag,
We would cheer fur Uncle Samuel an' the country
an' the flag.

Never had a bit o' trouble on the argumentive deal
Till ol' Poker Billy Davis made a quite disloyal
squeal
By a-sayin' that he soldiered fur the cause that's
vanished hence,
An' he's never liked a Yankee wuth a continental
sence.
He had hit the bowl that mornin' in a too extensive
way,
Which undoubtedly accounted fur his wild an' fatal
play;
Fur his craziness resulted in the diggin' of a hole,
An' a mortuary drama, — William in the leadin' role.

We jes' grabbed the boozy blower, an' we run him
to the bar,
An' we made him drink a swaller to each indivijul
star

PATRIOTISM AT SQUAWVILLE.

On the flag he had insulted, till we filled him to the
  throat,
An' till every vital organ in his system was afloat.
Sich a load o' liquid pizen would have killed an army
  mule,
Which was what the stuff accomplished fur the
  Yankee-hatin' fool,
An' the only one that mourned him was ol' Crazy
  Jane McGill,
Her that runs the boardin' shanty, whom the same he
  owed a bill.

— Denver Post.

The Guardsman.

MY brother Jim, he's in the regiment, an' he
  Says he's goin' down to fight
Soon as the soldiers ever start, an' gee !
  Maybe they'll go to-night !
He's got a suit just like a p'liceman, too,
  An' soldier cap an' gun.
He says they'll show the folks what they can do,
  He thinks it'll be fun !

But ma, she says she don't want him to go,
  'Cause she's afraid, I guess.
An' so, las' night she was a-cryin' so
  When Jim said that unless
She'd want to have a coward for a son
  He'd have to go an' fight,
That seemed just like she never would get done,
  But cried an' cried all night.

An' sis told Jim that if they went away
  She thought it was a shame,
An' cried when Jim said 'twas a lucky day
  To show that we are game ;
Sis liked Jim in his suit an' cap, an' so
  I thought she wouldn't care,

But she took on an' cried just like as though
  He's goin' to die down there!

But pa, you know he never said a word,
  Just like he couldn't talk.
But just shook hands with Jim, like this, real
     hard,
  An' went to take a walk;
An' bimeby I went out to try an' meet
  The kids, you know, an' do
Something, an' pa was walkin' up the street,
  An' he was cryin', too.

             —Frank X. Finnegan.

The Voice of the Oregon.

YOU have called to me, my brothers, from your
  far-off eastern sea,
To join with you, my brothers, to set a prostrate
  people free.
You have called to me, my brothers, to join to yours
  my might,
The slaughterers of our brethren with our armored
  hands to smite.

We have never met, my brothers, we mailed knights
  of the sea;
But there are no strangers, brothers, 'neath the Banner of the Free;
And though half a world's between us, and ten
  thousand leagues divide,
Our souls are intermingled, and our hearts are side
  by side.

Did you fail to call me, brothers, 'twere a fault
  without atone,
'Twas but just to me, my brothers, you should not
  strike alone.

THE VOICE OF THE OREGON.

The brethren in the slaughter were no more thine
    than mine,
And the blows that visit vengeance must be mine
    as well as thine.

Through days of placid beauty, and nights when
    tempests toss,
I follow down the billows, my guide the Southern
    Cross;
Past lands of quiet splendor, where pleasant waters
    lave;
Past lands whose mountain ramparts fling back the
    crashing wave.

But I see no land of splendor, and I see no land
    of wrath;
I see before me only the ocean's heaving path,
And I plunge along that pathway like a giant to the
    fray,
Who hath no stomach in him for aught that might
    delay.

I am nearing you, my brothers, for the western sea's
    afar,
And the ray that lights my course now is the gleam-
    ing Northern Star.

I pray you wait, my brothers, for the air with war is
    rife,
And in courtesy of knighthood I claim to share the
    strife.

In the winds that blow about me the voices of the
    dead
Are calling to me, brothers, to urge my topmost
    speed.
In the foam that's upward flying in whirling wreaths
    of white,
The wraiths of murdered brothers beckon onward
    to the fight.

I am coming to you, brothers, wait but a little while,
And on the thunders of our greeting shall the God
    of Vengeance smile;
And in the flashing and the crashing, the universe
    shall see
How we pay our debts of honor, we mailed knights
    of the sea.

—H. J. D. Browne.

War Poem.

STRIKE for the Anglo-Saxon !
  Strike for the Newer Day !
Oh, strike for Heart, and strike for
      Brain,
  And sweep the Beast away.

Not only for our sailors,
  The heroes of the *Maine*,
But strike for all the victims
  Of Moloch-minded Spain.

Not only for the Present,
  But all the Bloody Past,
Oh, strike for all the martyrs
  That have their hour at last.

Old stronghold of the Darkness,
  Come, ruin it with light !
It is no fight of small revenge,
  'Tis an immortal fight.

Spain is an ancient dragon,
  That all too long hath curled
Its coils of blood and darkness
  About the new-born world.

Think of the Inquisition !
  Think of the Netherlands !
Yea, think of all Spain's bloody deeds
  In many times and lands.

And let no feeble pity
  Your sacred arms restrain.
This is God's mighty moment
  To make an end of Spain.

     — Richard La Gallienne.

The Volunteer.

THE band was playing " Dixie " when he marched,
  marched away ;
An' never any likelier lad stept time to it that day ;
" The finest fellow of 'em all!" I heard the town-
  folk say.
The band was playin' " Dixie " as he marched,
  marched away.

How fast my wild arms held him, — my boy, who
  would not stay, —
The likeliest lad that answered to the captain's call
  that day!
" The finest fellow of 'em all!" An' in the red array
Of flags that rippled over them they marched my
  lad away!

But a mother's fears and prayers and tears were
  nothing. War must slay,
And the draped, deep drums were muffled as they
  brought him home that day!
" The finest fellow of 'em all!" I heard the town-
  folk say,
And his mother bendin' over him, — dead at her feet
  that day !

— Frank L. Stanton.

Regiment Song.

THE old flag is a-doin' of her very level best, —
    She's a rainbow roun' the country from the
    rosy east to west;
An' the eagle's in the elements with sunshine on his
    breast,
    An' we're marchin' with the country in the
    mornin'!

We're marchin' to the music that is ringin' fur an
    nigh;
You kin hear the hallelujahs as the regiments go by;
We'll live for this old country, or in Freedom's cause
    we'll die, —
    We're marchin' with the country in the mornin'!
                                    — *Frank L. Stanton.*

A Peace=at=any=price Man.

"WAR is coming! Blood must flow!" —
    Mary, get my satchel packed —
" We must meet the craven foe!" —
    Mary, get my satchel packed —
"There are wrongs that we must right.
Freeborn men, prepare to fight;
'Tis no time for childish fright" —
    Mary, get my satchel packed!

" Now let all the world give ear" —
    Mary, get my satchel packed —
" We've begged for war for half a year" —
    Mary, get my satchel packed —
" The President, at last, is stirred!
We have spoken, — he has heard, —
Now, then, for the final word" —
    Mary, get my satchel packed!

Clouds of war obscure the sky" —
    Mary, get my satchel packed —
Cuba's hope is mounting high" —
    Mary, get my satchel packed —

" Let our tars prepare to fight,
    Let them battle for the right " –
I start for Halifax to-night,
    Mary, get my satchel packed !

— *Baltimore Life*

Uncle Sam's Spring Cleaning.

"THERE has been a heap of rubbish dumped
about the patient seas,
And all cleaning hitherto has been a sham;
It is time for my spring cleaning, — and I hope you
catch my meaning, —
For I'm going to clean 'em out," says Uncle
Sam.
" And I'm going to rinse 'em down,
And I'm going to soak 'em out,
And I'm going to sponge 'em off, and make 'em
clean;
And I'll do a handsome job with my scrubbing
brush and swab,
And I'll give a different aspect to the scene.

" On the Philippines, a dumpground for the mediæ-
val truck,
And the old miasmal rubbish heaps of Spain,
I began my vernal cleaning, — and I think they
know my meaning, —
For I turned my hose upon them at full strain,
And I guess I swabbed 'em down,
And I guess I rubbed it in,

And I guess I swashed 'em off, and made 'em
    clean;
  And when I've wiped 'em dry with my army mop,
     says I,
There'll be a different aspect to the scene.

"And I'll clean off Porto Rico, and I'm going to
    wipe it dry,
  And poor filth-infested Cuba must be clean;
Four hundred years of lumber that its rubbish holes
    encumber, —
  If you wait you'll see it burn like kerosene.
And I guess I'll soap 'em down,
And I guess I'll scour 'em off,
And I guess I'll turn my hose on at full strain;
  And then, when I am through, then old Cuba will
    be new,
And there won't be any rubbish heaps of Spain.

"She has blotted all the oceans, and I'll wipe her
    off the seas,
  And I'll cleanse the cluttered islands of her slime;
And this is just the meaning of my vigorous spring
    cleaning, —
  Fate's washing day has come, — and it is time!
And I guess when I have soaped 'em,

UNCLE SAM'S SPRING CLEANING.

And I guess when I have wrung 'em,
And I guess when I have hung 'em out to dry,
  Not a single blot of Spain on an island shall
    remain,
And think that they'll feel cleaner then, says I."

— *Sam Walter Foss.*

The Phantoms.

THE phantom sea serenely blue
　　Beneath the sunshine lay,
And bold Cervera sailed his ships
　　Through clouds of phantom spray;
With phantom skill he steered his fleet
　　For many a phantom day.

One phantom morn the lookout cried,
　　"A sail!　I see a sail!"
The bold Cervera, undismayed,
　　Turned 'round, and then turned pale;
Then tried to turn the subject, and
　　Concluded to turn tail.

But closer to Cervera drew
　　That strangely foreign craft;
" Is she a Yank?" Cervera cried;
　　For answer phantom laught-
Er rolled across the phantom foam,
　　Like merriment gone daft.

" Wie gehts, alretty, vonce again!"
　　Came to Cervera's ear;
" Ve haf peen looging ouid py you
　　Dis many und many a year;

THE PHANTOMS.

Und now, py Chimineddy, ve
   Are glat to see you here!"

"Oh, who are you?" Cervera cried,
   With terror in each tone.
"I vos der Flying Dutchman, yet!"
   Came through the megaphone;
"Und I am glat dot nefermore
   I'll sail der sea alone."

And so, across the phantom deep,
   And through the phantom spray,
Through phantom storms, and phantom
      calms,
   Through phantom night and day,
The Flying Dutchman and the Fly-
   Ing Spaniard sail for aye.
          —*Baltimore News.*

The Heroic Dead.

THEY are not dead whose names we
    breathe
  With trembling voice and tear-dimmed
    eyes,
For whom the marble shaft we wreathe
  With garlands of immortal dyes;
Not dead, — they sleep, while angel guards
  Patrol their camp on every hand;
Sweet rest at last their toil rewards
  Who sought to save their leaguered land.

When Liberty assailed, oppressed,
  Raised up her voice against the wrong,
O loyal sons of dauntless breast,
  How firm ye stood in cordon strong.
A hero's soul in every eye
  Fired with a hero's purpose grand,
For liberty, if need, to die,
  Or, living, for her cause to stand.

The screaming shot, the bursting shell,
  The long-roll echoing through the night,
To lead the charge 'mid groan and yell,
  The deadly struggle might with might.

THE HEROIC DEAD.

The bivouac on the bloody field
   Racked with the pangs of wounds and
      thirst,
Too weak to fly — too brave to yield —
   With bitterness of death accurst.

The horrors of the prison pen,
   Whence few who entered ever came,
Starvation in a loathsome den
   Where life was death and hope a name;
All these and more these heroes dared
   That freedom's light might shine afar,
Each breast to death was freely bared
   Amid the wild alarm of war.

Again across Columbia's plains
   The war trump peals its thrilling blast,
Once more it sings in stirring strains
   The glorious triumphs of the past;
The answering tread of mustering hosts,
   The land aglow with bivouac fires,
Proclaim that still our Union boasts
   Sons brave and loyal as their sires.

These graves with tears of love bedew,
   And deck them with the bloom of May
In honor of the boys in blue,
   In memory of the boys in gray.

No more opposed in deadly strife,
  Brother to brother, sire to son,
They proved their valor life for life,
  Now side by side they sleep, — as one.

Sleep on, brave hearts, and take your rest,
  A hundred million strong and free
Shall guard in each heroic breast
· Your pure and priceless legacy.
'Twas not in vain, O noble band,
  Your blood imbued Columbia's sod,
United now her children stand, —
  One flag, one country, and one God.

                    —*Geo. D. Emery.*

Strike the Blow.

THE four-way winds of the world have blown,
  And the ships have ta'en the wave;
The legions march to the trumps' shrill call
  'Neath the flag of the free and brave.
    The hounds of the sea
    Have trailed the foe,
    They have trailed and tracked him down, —
      Then wait no longer, but strike, O land,
      With the dauntless strength of thy strong
        right hand,
      Strike the blow!

The armored fleets, with their grinning guns,
  Have the Spaniard in his lair;
They have tracked him down where the ramparts
    frown,
  And they'll halt and hold him there.
    They have steamed in his wake,
    They have seen him go,
    They have bottled and corked him up;
      Then send him home to the underfoam,
      Till the wide sea shakes to the far blue
        dome;
      Strike the blow!

The Cuban dead and the dying call,
 The children starved in the light
Of the aid that waits till the hero deed
 Breaks broad on the tyrant's might.
  The starved and the weak
   In their hour of woe
  Are calling, land, on thee;
   Then why delay in thy dauntless sway?
   On, on, to the charge of the freedom-way,
   Strike the blow!

They have ta'en the winds of the Carib seas,
 Thy fleets that know not fear;
Their ribs of steel have yearned to reel
 In the dance of the cannoneer.
  Thy sons of the blue
   That wait to go
  Would leap with a will to the charge,
   Then send them the word so long deferred;
   They have listened late, but they have not
    heard;
   Strike the blow!

They have listened late in the desolate land,
 They have looked through brimming eyes,
And starving women have held dead babes
 To their heart with a thousand sighs.

STRIKE THE BLOW.

On, on to the end,
   O land, the foe
Beneath thy sword shall fall,
   Thy ships of steel have tracked them home,
   Ye are king of the land and king of the foam.
   Strike the blow!

— F. McK.

Hold Dot Fort, for We Vos Coming.

HAUL in der plank, full speed ahead, —
   Undt so dose shteamers sailed avay,
Undt tears undt prayers dose ships go mit,
   Undt aching hearts pehind dem shtay.
Vhen dose ships pass der Golden Gate,
   Undt dot Pacific's swell dey feel,
Vat strike deir pows, vat lap deir sides,
   Undt quiver dem from truck to keel,

Say, den a chill vos in mein plood,
   I lifd mein eyes oop to der sky,
Undt from each ship vat sailed avay,
   I see Old Glory masthead high.
" Mein Gott," I cried, " I vos olt mans,
   But nefer I see dot pefore,
Dot Yankee ships mit soltjer poys
   Vos sailing for a foreign shore."

Mit swords undt peestols, undt mit guns, —
   Mit all war's horrid tools dey go.
To haf a picnic? — No, mein Gott,
   To pattle mit a foreign foe.

HOLD DOT FORT, FOR VE VOS COMING.

I'd gif von halluf ov mein life,
   Ohf by Manila I could shtand,
Vhen Dewey hear dose vistles scream,
   Undt Merritt shake dot hero's hand.

Some kings vat lif across der sea —
   Undt Emp'ror Villiam he vos one —
Dey shpeak mean dings der Yankees ov,
   Undt Villiam he haf blendy fun.
Vell, Villiam, all your poys vat lif
   In Yankee land, dey vos true blue,
But in der faderland — oh, vell —
   When Shpain vos licked ve shpeak mit
      you.
           — Hans Von Dunkerfoodle.

The Spaniard Answered.

The Americans are a cowardly race. — *Spanish Newspaper.*

WE are not a warlike nation; here of old our
  fathers settled,
  Seeking scope for their opinions, in the log house
    and the hut;
Seeking elbow room and freedom, sober men and
    quiet mettled,
  Almost too religious, maybe, peaceful-minded peo-
    ple; but —

Since they wished to farm the meadows, wished to
    go to church on Sunday,
  And the redskin would annoy them with his lust
    for human hair,
From far Georgia to the south'ard, to the misty shore
    of Fundy,
  Flintlocks kept the plough a-going, bullets helped
    to speed the prayer.

We are not a warlike nation; though the blood we
    brought was ruddy,
  We preferred its cherry runnels in the veins kept
    tightly shut.

We had thews for farm and fishnet; we had brains
    to scheme and study;
  Brawn and brain for peace and quiet, — that was
    all we wanted; but —

Ask the fields of sleepy Concord, ask old wrecked
    Ticonderoga,
  Of the cost of unjust taxes and old bottles for new
    wine!
Something more than glass was broken on the heights
    of Saratoga,
  And the tax was paid at Yorktown by the stiff old
    buff-blue line.

We are not a warlike nation; patterned, rather, for
    keen trading;
  Some will say the style is English, that from them
    we get the cut;
East and west our ships went speeding, decks awash
    from heavy lading,
  Bowsprits poked in every harbor, never seeking
    quarrels; but —

When our rich Levant trade came, and Tripoli
    claimed tribute from it, —
  Tribute paid by other navies trading down the
    midland sea, —

We, the least and last of nations, blew her gunboats
    to Mahomet,
  Blew the faithful to their houris, made the straits
    forever free.

We are not a warlike nation; we had states to form
    and settle,
  We had stuffs to manufacture, till our markets
    felt the glut;
We were busy getting headway, busy panning out
    the metal
  From the human dust that reached us from the
    old-world digging; but —

We could slow up for a moment, just to show our
    elder brother
  That the bird we put our faith in was not stuffed
    upon his perch;
And we told him through the cannon, in the sea
    fights' reek and smother,
  We had searched the Scripture duly, but had
    found no " right to search."

We are not a warlike nation; peace sometimes keeps
    men's souls sleeping;
  Some of us still sought our harvests in the old
    barbaric rut

Worn by captive feet, till, one day, party feeling
    upward leaping,
  Broke into a flame and blazed on all the startled
    nations; but —

When the smoke from red fields lifted, when the
    armies were disbanded, —
  Better armies, all the world knows, never cartridge
    bit or rammed, —
Proud of their own deeds, and proud, too, of the men
    who, lighter handed,
  Fought them long and ofttimes whipped them,
    slavery was dead and damned.

We are not a warlike nation; we love life far more
    than dying;
  We have little time for swagger and the military
    strut;
Let old Europe pay big armies; we have better fish
    for frying,
  We have nobler tools for manhood than the sword
    and rifle; but —

Since we are a Christian nation, and the blood our
    veins are filled with —
  Anglo-Saxon, Celtic, Teuton — will not keep for-
    ever cool,

When we see weak women starving, helpless, ill-
    starred children killed with
  Filthy water, air empoisoned, just to eke out Span-
    ish rule ;

Since we find that Cuba's Cuban, and the Spaniard
    but a tenant
  Who defiles the house he lives in, then our duty
    stands out plain ;
We are masters in these waters, at the mainmast
    flies our pennant,
  End this hell on earth, or, hark ye, eastward lies
    the path to Spain !
                     — *Robert Cameron Rogers.*

A Song for the Fleet.

A SONG for them one and all,
   The sister-ships of the *Maine*,
They have sailed at a nation's battle-call
To save a land from a tyrant's thrall
   That has struggled long in vain!

The coming days shall speak
   The praise of our valiant tars!
No fear they will wanting prove, or weak,
When proudly flutters from every peak
   The glorious stripes and stars!

Then cheer for the flag unfurled
   On the dawn of that Sabbath day,
When the shot that the gallant Dewey hurled
Crushed the hopes of the Spanish world,
   In the far Manila Bay!

And a cheer for the valorous ones
   Who are girt for the gory fight,
Where the tropic tide-race swirls and runs
Under the frown of the Morro's guns —
   And God be with the right!

          — *Clinton Scollard.*

War Hymn.

OH, rise up in your glorious might,
    America, America!
Destroy the wrong, defend the right,
    America, America!
Oh, see the pleading hand outheld,
Behold the fetters tyrants weld;
And shall thine aid be still withheld?
    America, America!

Thy sons are loyal, brave, and true,
    America, America!
They're burning now to dare and do,
    America, America!
No brother looks to thee in vain;
We'll crush the power of cruel Spain;
Remembered be the martyred *Maine*.
    America, America!

Then give three cheers for Dewey, true,
    America, America!
And for the grand Red, White, and Blue,
    America, America!

WAR HYMN.

Our ships are victors on the sea,
And Cuba shall be, must be free!
All honor do we give to thee,
     America, America!
           —Beulah R. Stevens.

The Soarin' o' the Eagle.

OH, we met the Spanish squadron
  In the choppy China Sea;
With "Old Glory" up above us,
  And our Commodore Dewey;
And a brace of Yankee seamen
(Every fightin' tar a freeman) —
And the way we trounced the haughty Dons
  Was beautiful to see.

We shelled 'em out to seaward, —
  And we shelled 'em on the shore;
And we trained our guns to leeward
  For a hundred shots or more;
For the rag that hung above us,
And the Yankee hearts that love us —
Why, we made the eagle hump himself
  And show 'em how to soar.

Oh, the decks was slippin' bloody,
  And the guns was smokin' hot;
And the centre o' the scrimmage
  Was an interestin' spot;
And the beggars kept salutin'
In a disrespectful shootin'

THE SOARIN' O' THE EAGLE.

Till we sent 'em Yankee manners
 In a dozen ton of shot.

Our ears was full o' cotton,
 And our legs was all a-reel;
But the Yankee grit was in us,
 And our guns was full o' steel;
And we kept the Greasers hoppin'
With the shells that we was droppin'
Till we filled 'em full o' blazin' hell
 From reekin' deck to keel.

Oh, we bored 'em full o' trouble
 As a sieve is full o' holes;
And we chucked 'em under water
 Like a nest o' drownded moles.
With the blessin' o' Saint Mary
And the Yankee military —
Why, we give 'em twenty volleys
 For the restin' o' their souls.

They fought us square and honest,
 And they spoiled our purty shine;
And they went down game as chickens
 When we sunk 'em in the brine;
For while the eagle's screamin',
And the stars and stripe's a-streamin',

Why, we hain't the boys to say it, —
That they didn't toe the line.

Oh, they thought they'd have a bull-fight
With your Uncle Sammy's crew ;
And they figgered out that dodgin'
Was the proper thing to do.
But they missed their calculation
In a-sizin' up the nation, —
Cause there hain't no room fer Spaniards
When the eagle soars the blue.

      — *Marion Franklin Ham.*

The Call to the Colors.

" ARE you ready, O Virginia,
       Alabama, Tennessee?
People of the Southland, answer!
    For the land hath need of thee."
" Here!" from sandy Rio Grande,
    Where the Texan horsemen ride;
" Here!" the hunters of Kentucky
    Hail from Chatterawha's side;
Every toiler in the cotton,
    Every rugged mountaineer,
Velvet-voiced and iron-handed,
    Lifts his head to answer, " Here!
Some remain who charged with Pickett,
    Some survive who followed Lee;
They shall lead their sons to battle
    For the flag, if need there be."

" Are you ready, California,
    Arizona, Idaho?
' Come, oh, come, unto the colors!'
    Heard you not the bugle blow?"
Falls a hush in San Francisco
    In the busy hives of trade;

In the vineyards of Sonoma
  Fall the pruning knife and spade;
In the mines of Colorado
  Pick and drill are thrown aside;
Idly in Seattle harbor
  Swing the merchants to the tide;
And a million mighty voices
  Throb responsive like a drum,
Rolling from the rough Sierras,
  " You have called us, and we come."

O'er Missouri sounds the challenge —
  O'er the great lakes and the plain;
" Are you ready, Minnesota?
  Are you ready, men of Maine?"
From the woods of Ontonagon,
  From the farms of Illinois,
From the looms of Massachusetts,
  " We are ready, man and boy."
Axemen free, of Androscoggin,
  Clerks who trudge the cities' paves,
Gloucester men who drag their plunder
  From the sullen, hungry waves,
Big-boned Swede and large-limbed
        German,
  Celt and Saxon swell the call,

THE CALL TO THE COLORS.

And the Adirondacks echo:
  "We are ready, one and all."

Truce to feud and peace to faction!
  All forgot is party zeal
When the war-ships clear for action,
  When the blue battalions wheel.
Europe boasts her standing armies, —
  Serfs who blindly fight by trade;
We have seven million soldiers,
  And a soul guides every blade.
Laborers with arm and mattock,
  Laborers with brain and pen,
Railroad prince and railroad brakeman
  Build our line of fighting men.
Flag of righteous wars! close mustered
  Gleam the bayonets, row on row,
Where thy stars are sternly clustered,
  With their daggers towards the foe.

          — New York Mail and Express.

Remembered.

FROM Cuban shores in ceaseless pain,
  Out of the calling sea,
Long cried the Spirit of the *Maine*,
  " Will ye remember me ? "

At last the laggard answer comes
  From 'neath the Eastern suns,
Borne westward on the thundering roll,
  The deep song of the guns.

From where the war winds shrieked and
      sang,
  The battle bugles blew,
And deathless names in history sprang,
  Proud as man ever knew.

Comes the wild, wailing voice of Spain, —
  While o'er her war-ships stir
Such waves as wash the martyred *Maine*, —
  " Ye have remembered her ! "

                    —*James Lindsay Gordon.*

300

𝕬 𝔖ong for t𝔥e 𝔥our.

L ET Tyranny tremble and Cowardice quake,
    The people have spoken, — their flag is un-
      furled,
And now for our God and humanity's sake,
    Let Mars' mighty thunders awaken the world.

The sobs of the suffering appeal not in vain;
    Columbia has lifted her radiant shield,
And it's woe to despotic and blood-shedding Spain,
    When Freedom's brave knighthood has taken the
      field.

The wrath of the Nation is kindled at last,
    And Liberty's light shall illumine the sky,
The Faith of our fathers, that hallows our past,
    Proclaims from their dust that the despot must
      die.

No longer we parley with tyrants for truce;
    Let the war-drum make music to clashing of
      steel, —
The eagle has screamed and the war-dogs are
      loose, —
    And it's woe to Havana and woe to Castile.

                — *William F. Dunbar.*

A Message.

To the men who fought with Decatur,
  To the men who with Lawrence died,
To the men who fell in that blazing hell
  Of Mobile by Farragut's side;
Take to them our message stern and plain,
Tell them the guns are cast loose again,
      Men of the *Maine !*

This to the men of the ships of oak
  From the men of the ships of steel,
To the hearts that broke 'mid the flame and
      smoke
  From the living hearts that feel,
There is no mizzen, nor fore, nor main,
But all of the flags are aloft again,
      Men of the *Maine !*

Not against foes of our own true blood,
  Nor kin across the sea,
But straight in the face of a stranger race
  Who never, like you, were free.
Tell them 'tis thus that our guns we train,
And the sights are lined, and the strings astrain,
      Men of the *Maine !*

A MESSAGE.

Take them these tidings, ye who sleep
   'Neath the murky waves by the Cuban town,
The blow in the night but began the fight
   Which ends when the Spanish flag comes
      down,
And our guns shall thunder their old refrain
Tolling your knell from here — to Spain!
     Men of the *Maine !*

                — *P. B.*

In the Time of Strife.

WE may not know
    How red the lilies of the spring shall grow;
      What silver flood,
Sea-streaming, take the crimson tints of blood.

    We may not know
If victory shall make the bugles blow;
      If still shall wave
The flag above our freedom or our grave.

    We only know
One heart, one hand, one country, meet the foe;
      On land and sea
Her liegemen in the battle of the free.
                  — Frank L. Stanton.

The Martyrs of the Maine.

AND they have thrust our shattered dead away in
    foreign graves,
Exiled forever from the port the homesick sailor
    craves!
    They trusted once in Spain,
    They're trusting her again!
    And with the holy care of our own sacred slain!
    No, no, the Stripes and Stars
    Must wave above our tars.
                Bring them home!

On a thousand hills the darling dead of all our battles
    lie
In nooks of peace, with flowers and flags, but now
    they seem to cry
    From out their bivouac:
    "Here every good man Jack
    Belongs.   Nowhere but here — with us.
    So bring them back."
    And on the Cuban gales
    A ghostly rumor wails,
                "Bring us home!"

305

Poltroon, the people that neglects to guard the bones,
    the dust,
The reverenced relics its warriors have bequeathed in
    trust!
    But heroes, too, were these
    Who sentinel'd the seas
    And gave their lives to shelter us in careless
      ease.
    Shall we desert them, slain,
    And proffer them to Spain
    As alien mendicants, — these martyrs of our
      Maine?
           No! Bring them home!
               — Rupert Hughes.

Dies Irae.

WHERE is the heritage that once was Spain's —
  Half the proud world with endless riches
    piled?
Ah, all hath vanished; nothing now remains
  Save one sad island, — one unhappy child, —

Cuba, last daughter of the Western seas,
  Gaunt victim of the she-wolf's ruthless spoil,
Whose piteous moans rise on each passing breeze,
  While drop by drop her life-blood damps the soil.

Four hundred years! God's vengeance tarrieth late;
  And yet, at last! the day of wrath hath come;
Columbia, bare thy steel! The nations wait
  To see thee drive the keen-edged weapon home!

Those Rebel Flags.

Discussed by " One of the Yanks."

SHALL we send back the Johnnies their bunting,
In token, from Blue to the Gray,
That " Brothers-in-blood " and " Good Hunting "
Shall be our new watchword to-day?
In olden times knights held it knightly
To return to brave foemen the sword;
Will the Stars and the Stripes gleam less
brightly
If the old Rebel flags are restored?

Call it sentiment, call it misguided
To fight to the death for " a rag; "
Yet, trailed in the dust, derided,
The true soldier still loves his flag!
Does love die, and must honor perish
When colors and causes are lost?
Lives the soldier who ceases to cherish
The blood-stains and valor they cost?

Our battle-fields, safe in the keeping
Of Nature's kind, fostering care,

Are blooming, — our heroes are sleeping, —
   And peace broods perennial there.
All over our land rings the story
   Of loyalty, fervent and true ;
" One flag," and that flag is " Old Glory,"
   Alike for the Gray and the Blue.

Why cling to those moth-eaten banners ?
   What glory or honor to gain
While the nation is shouting hosannas,
   Uniting her sons to fight Spain ?
Time is ripe, and the harvest worth reaping,
   Send the Johnnies their flags f. o. b.,
Address to the care and safe-keeping
   Of that loyal " old Reb," Fitzhugh Lee !

Yes, send back the Johnnies their bunting,
   With greetings from Blue to the Gray ;
We are " Brothers-in-blood," and " Good
      Hunting "
   Is America's watchword to-day.
                      —*John H. Jewett.*

Britannia to Columbia.

WHAT is the voice I hear
    On the wind of the Western sea?
Sentinel, listen from out Cape Clear,
    And say what the voice may be.
" 'Tis a proud, free people calling loud to a people
    proud and free.

" And it says to them, ' Kinsmen, hail!
    We severed have been too long;
Now let us have done with a worn-out tale,
    The tale of an ancient wrong,
And our friendship last long as love doth last, and
    be stronger than death is strong.' "

Answer them, sons of the selfsame race,
    And blood of the selfsame clan,
Let us speak with each other, face to face,
    And answer as man to man,
And loyally love and trust each other as none but
    free men can.

Now fling them out to the breeze,
    Shamrock, thistle, and rose,

And the Star Spangled Banner unfurl with these,
    A message to friends and foes,
Wherever the sails of peace are seen, and wherever
    the war wind blows.

A message to bond and thrall to wake,
    For wherever we come, we twain,
The throne of the tyrant shall rock and quake
    And his menace be void and vain,
For you are lords of a strong young land and we are
    lords of the main.

Yes, this is the voice on the bluff March gale,
    " We severed have been too long;
But now we have done with a worn-out tale,
    The tale of an ancient wrong,
And our friendship shall last long as love doth last,
    and be stronger than death is strong."

                                 —*Alfred Austin.*

Chickamauga — 1898.

THEY are camped on Chickamauga!
  Once again the white tents gleam
On that field where vanished heroes
  Sleep the sleep that knows no dream.
There are shadows all about them
  Of the ghostly troops to-day,
But they light the common camp-fire, —
  Those who wore the blue and gray.

Where the pines of Georgia tower,
  Where the mountains kiss the sky,
On their arms the Nation's warriors
  Wait to hear the battle-cry.
Wait together, friends and brothers,
  And the heroes 'neath their feet
Sleep the long and dreamless slumber
  Where the flowers are blooming sweet.

Sentries pause, yon shadow challenge!
  Rock-ribbed Thomas goes that way, —
He who fought the foe unyielding
  In that awful battle fray.
Yonder pass the shades of heroes,
  And they follow where Bragg leads

CHICKAMAUGA — 1898.

Through the meadows and the river, —
　But no ghost the sentry heeds.

Field of fame, a patriot army
　Treads thy sacred sod to-day!
And they'll face a common foeman,
　Those who wore the blue and gray,
And they'll fight for common country,
　And they'll charge to victory
'Neath the folds of one brave banner, —
　Starry banner of the free!

They are camped off Chickamauga,
　Where the green tents of the dead
Turn the soil into a glory
　Where a Nation's heart once bled;
But they're clasping hands together
　On this storied field of strife, —
Brothers brave who meet to battle
　In the freedom-war of life!

—Baltimore News.

Chickamauga.

1863.

FROM shuddering trees the painted leaves
  Strew redder dyes of crimson sod;
And brave men lie in ghastly sheaves,
  As whirled there by the wrath of God.
Gray vapors hum with wings of death,
  Whose roll-call speeds its fierce alarms;
And life sighs, "Here!" with parting breath,
  Where bleeding thousands ground their arms.
For brothers face each other's steel,
Grim suitors in the last appeal.

1898.

From laughing leas the bugles sing,
  More shrill than bird to nesting mate
O'er tented slopes the war notes ring,
  And time again the tramp of fate.
Bright oriflamme of liberty,
  Our bannered blazon flaunts the sky,
And hails the "sun-burst" in the sea,
  A gallant people's anguished cry.
Now, brothers, touch in common weal
To right that foreign wrong with steel.

— G. T. Ferris.

One Beneath Old Glory.

DON'T you hear the tramp of soldiers?
  Don't you hear the bugles play?
Don't you see the muskets flashing
  In the sunlight far away?
Don't you feel the ground all trembling
  'Neath the tread of many feet?
They are coming, tens of thousands,
  To the army and the fleet.

They are Yankees, they are Johnnies,
  They're for North and South no more;
They are one, and glad to follow
  When Old Glory goes before.
From Atlantic to Pacific,
  From the Pine Tree to Lone Star,
They are gath'ring 'round Old Glory,
  And they're marching to the war.

Don't you see the harbors guarded
  By those bristling dogs of war?
Don't you hear them growling, barking,
  At the fleet beyond the bar?
Don't you hear the Jack Tars cheering,
  Brave as sailor lads can be?

315

Don't you see the water boiling
  Where the squadron put to sea?

They are Yankees, they are Johnnies,
  They're for North and South no more;
They are one, and glad to follow
  When Old Glory goes before.
From Atlantic to Pacific,
  From the Pine Tree to Lone Star,
They have gathered 'round Old Glory,
  And they're sailing to the war.

Don't you hear the horses prancing?
  Don't you hear the sabres clash?
Don't you hear the cannons roaring?
  Don't you hear the muskets crash?
Don't you smell the smoke of battle?
  Oh, you'll wish that you had gone,
When you hear the shouts and cheering
  For the boys who whipped the Don!

There'll be Yankees, there'll be Johnnies,
  There'll be North and South no more,
When the boys come marching homeward
  With Old Glory borne before.
From Atlantic to Pacific,
  From the Pine Tree to Lone Star,
They'll be one beneath Old Glory
  After coming from the war.

The Maine.

BRAVE hearts still'd on the *Maine*, a last
 good night!
Good night to gallant fellowship and stanch
Lives, not less honor'd if not lost in fight!
 Tho' upon unknown waters ye must launch
Your boats with our rich cargo of regret,
 None who our country love can bid good-by
To your remembrance, nor can e'er forget
 What sacrifice ye made for her.   We die
In age 'mid aliens, but in youth 'mid friends
 Whose impulses are ours, to whom alike
The bright meridian of manhood lends
 Its glory.   Tho' your knell untimely strike,
No silent silting of the hurried years
May hide your worth, nor choke the source of
 tears!   — *Griswald Dichter.*

A Song for the Sailor-men.

NOW it's hail to the commander,
 And it's hail the valiant fleet!
And it's hail the guns that thundered
 Through the battle's lurid heat!
But we'll not forget the sailors,
 So it's sailor-men, hurrah!
It's your country's hand we give you,
 For to shake your grimy paw.

The sailor-men, the sailor-men,
 The men who fought below,
The gunners and the striplings
 And the navvies we don't know —
But it's hail to them, and Honor
 Wreath her roses 'round their fame;
For 'twas them that did their duty
 When the cannon spoke their flame!

Oh, cheer the mighty commodore, —
 The credit is his due, —
And cheer the under officers,
 The gunners and the crew!
But don't forget the sailor-men,
 Who fought the fight below,

A SONG FOR THE SAILOR-MEN.

Where the devil lit his furnace,
   And they hadn't any show.

The sailor-men, the sailor-men,
   A flag we'll fly for them,
And the girls will wreath the roses
   In a gaudy diadem,
For to crown the seaman's valor,
   And to honor them that sweat
Where the devil lights his furnace
   And the bloody decks are wet.

Now it's hail unto the commodore,
   The captains, and all that!
But we sha'n't forget the underlings,
   Or be they Mike or Pat;
For they fought the fight with valor —
   Here's your country's hand to you,
Every hearty lad that's numbered
   In the squadron's noble crew.

The sailor-men, the sailor-men,
   The lowest and the high,
With a heart for any duty, —
   Though that duty be to die, —
Here's a cheer across the valleys,
   And an echo o'er the hills;

For the land from hill to valley
  With your splendid triumph thrills!

Yea, hail the grimy sailor-man, —
  And sure he's got a breast
That is filled with love of country, —
  And it's hail him with the rest,
For the fires he kept a-burning,
  And the guns he kept awake,
And the sweet life that he offered
  For his darlin' country's sake!

Oh, the sailor-man, the sailor-man!
  When all is said and done,
At Manila or wherever
  Valor's bloody race is run,
He's deservin' of affection;
  For, behold, the commodore
Without the grimy sailor-man
  Can't make the cannon roar!

—*Baltimore News.*

In Days Like These.

O GOD of hosts, whose mighty hand
　　Our fathers led across the seas,
We took from thee our goodly land,
　　To thee we look in days like these.
'Mid swelling tumult, bitter word,
　　'Mid clashing arms and bugles' blare,
　　While war-drums fret the fevered air,
In days like these, be near, O Lord.

The winds have swept our colors out,
　　Our polished guns the sun has kissed;
With measured step and loyal shout,
　　The men trooped by who now are missed.
The hilltops signal far away,
　　And sea calls sea with beacon lips,
　　Where ride our far-flung battle ships,
To strike the foe at break of day.

Forgive, O Lord, that we forgot
　　To humble self and thee to please;
Our vows unkept, sins thought, unthought,
　　Forgive, O Lord, in days like these.
Our gift upon the altar lies,

Accept it ere thou call us hence,
Although thou saidst obedience
Is better than a sacrifice.

'Tis not for gain or vengeful spite
Our treasure and our life is poured,
But for the wronged who have no might,
Whose cry has reached the ear of God.
In days like these our motives take,
Since whom thou usest thou must trust;
And when we strike because we must,
Help us to heal the wounds we make.

— Thomas H. Stacy.

ℜemesis.

THE MAINE.

SHE glided on her peaceful quest,
  What though her starry flag might bear
To some a silent, stern behest,
  To some a breath of freedom's air;
Then in her berth, a stately guest,
  Slept, trustful, in that alien lair.

But what are bulkheads, fashioned well,
  And what are sides and decks of steel,
Or cunning dial-hands, to tell,
  Through night and day, of woe or weal,
When human hearts can league with hell
  And sow volcanoes 'neath a keel?

So, by a deed whose blackness made
  The night it chose seem white beside,
Struck in the dark by coward's blade,
  The knightly *Maine* leapt once and died, —
A name to make a throne afraid, —
  A wreck that moaned beneath the tide!

323

THE OREGON.

But o'er the land the tidings swept,
  And death-cries quivered through the wire;
Down in the hole the engines leapt,
  The coal sprang eager to the fire,
And never slacked and never slept
  The sister war-ship's grim desire!

With patient throbs that never wane
  A continent's long coast is won;
That nearing death-smoke on the main
  Shall teach the lesson to the Don
That he who strikes a blow at *Maine*
  Shall reckon yet with *Oregon!*

Ah, when her helm goes hard aport,
  And all her broadside speaks in fire,
And from the proudly floating fort
  The cheers ring out with brave desire,
That sound shall shake a trembling court,
  And thrill Havana's sunken pyre!
                                    — C. H. Crandall.

The War-ship "Dixie."

THEY'VE named a cruiser "Dixie,"— that's whut
    the papers say, —
An' I hears they're goin' to man her with the boys
    that wore the gray;
Good news! It sorter thrills me, an' makes me want
    ter be
Whar the ban' is playin' "Dixie," an' the *Dixie*
    puts ter sea!

They've named a cruiser "Dixie." An', fellers, I'll
    be boun'
You're goin' ter see some fightin' when the *Dixie*
    swings aroun'!
Ef any o' them Spanish ships shall strike her, east
    or west,
Jest let the ban' play "Dixie," an' the boys'll do the
    rest!

I want to see that *Dixie*, — I want ter take my stan'
On the deck of her and holler: "Three cheers fer
    Dixie lan'!"
She means we're all united, — the war hurts healed
    away,
An' "Way Down South in Dixie" is national to-day!

I bet you she's a good 'un! I'll stake my last red
    cent
Thar ain't no better timber in the whole blame settle-
    ment!
An' all their shiny battle-ships beside that ship air
    tame,
Fer, when it comes to " Dixie," thar's somethin' in
    a name!

Here's three cheers an' a tiger, — as hearty as kin be;
An' let the ban' play " Dixie " when the *Dixie* puts
    ter sea!
She'll make her way an' win the day from shinin' East
    to West —
Jest let the ban' play " Dixie," an' the boys'll do the
    rest.

                              — *Frank L. Stanton.*

The Eagle's Song.

THE lioness whelped, and the sturdy cub
   Was seized by an eagle, and carried up,
And homed for awhile in an eagle's nest,
And slept for awhile on an eagle's breast;
And the eagle taught it the eagle's song:
" To be stanch, and valiant, and free, and
       strong ! "

The lion whelp sprang from the eyrie nest,
From the lofty crag where the queen birds rest;
He fought the King on the spreading plain,
And drove him back o'er the foaming main.
He held the land as a thrifty chief,
And reared his cattle, and reaped his sheaf,
Nor sought the help of a foreign hand,
Yet welcomed all to his own free land !

Two were the sons that the country bore
To the Northern lakes and the Southern shore; ·
And Chivalry dwelt with the Southern son,
And Industry lived with the Northern one.
Tears for the time when they broke and fought !
Tears was the price of the union wrought !
And the land was red in a sea of blood,
Where brother for brother had swelled the flood !

And now that the two are one again,
Behold on their shield the word " Refrain ! "
And the lion cubs twain sing the eagle's song:
" To be stanch, and valiant, and free, and
      strong ! "
For the eagle's beak, and the lion's paw,
And the lion's fangs, and the eagle's claw,
And the eagle's swoop, and the lion's might,
And the lion's leap, and the eagle's sight,
Shall guard the flag with the word " Refrain ! "
Now that the two are one again!
          — *Richard Mansfield.*

The Dream of the Spanish Admiral.

A. D. 1541.

IN slumber as the morning broke
  (It was our homeward voyage to Spain)
Methought I gave a parting look
  At the New World beyond the main.
The shores were low, and soft and faint,
  Half purple mist and half firm land,
On which the sunbeams seemed to paint
  The semblance of a foamy strand.

I dreamed I saw a hundred ships
  Where not a sail had glanced before,
And for chained hands and livid lips
  I heard a new-born people roar.
To every mast a flag was nailed,
  No lion crest, but stripes and stars,
And deep into the sea they sailed
  To wrestle with us, old in wars.

They clove our ranks, they clomb the towers
  Our loftiest galleons proudly bore:
They struck with more than mortal powers,
  Till Spain herself could strike no more.

And down the wind we drifted far,
   And to the shore our hulks were blown;
The sea was thick with mast and spar,
   And Spain was shaken from her throne.

And louder than the whirring brine,
   And louder than the cannon's roar,
I heard a voice, " Vengeance is mine,
   I recompense for evermore ! "
Now may St. James defend us still,
   And may the cavaliers of Spain
Sail on and conquer whom they will,
   And teach me that my dream was vain.

                    — *Samuel Dorman.*

Just One Signal.

THE war-path is true and straight,
    It knoweth no left nor right;
Why ponder and wonder and vacillate?
    The way to fight is to fight.

The officer of the deck
    Had climbed to a perch aloft,
And he leaned far out and he craned his neck,
    And his tones were gentle and soft:
" I see," he whispered, " off there to port,
    Through the night shade's lesser black,
The darker blur of the outer fort,
    Preparing for the attack."
They signalled it so, and sharp and short
    The answer was signalled back:
        " Keep on."

Again from the upper air
    Came the quiet voice of the guide:
" The admiral's flagship's over there,
    Two miles on the starboard side.
It's a long, long way for the best of eyes,
    But I know her by moon and sun,

I know by her lines and I know her size —
  And there goes her warning gun."
" That boat will make a most excellent prize,"
  Said the admiral, " when we've won.
          Keep on."

The whispering came again:
  " I think by the hints and signs
Appearing ahead of us now and then
  That we're getting among their mines.
Ten fathom in front, as the searchlights show,
  I fancy that I can detect
The line of their outermost works — Ah, no !
  It is nearer than I'd suspect."
The message was sent to the admiral so,
  And he answered to this effect :
          " Keep on."

The haze of the dawning day
  Slid into the shades of night,
And he called : " Off there in the upper bay,
  They're lining their ships for a fight.
I think they are training on us — " No more
  He said, for the dawn was lit
By the blaze of a gun from the neighboring shore,

And he fell to the deck, hard hit.
They signalled: " The first man struck." As before
   The admiral answered it:
            " Keep on."

The sun came over the hills
   As wishing a world-wide weal.
And the guns were fired with the aim that kills,
   And steel pierced the heart of steel.
And the line of shore was the fringe of hell,
   And the centre of hell was the sea,
And the woe was the woe no tongue may tell,
   And no eye view tearlessly,
And over that crater of bomb and shell
   The signal continued to be:
            " Keep on."

O Lawrence, whose passing cry
   Grows ever the more sublime,
And thou, O Nile king, whose words shall die
   When we learn of the death of time,
We send you the third of a glorious three;
   We send you a battle shout
That echoes up from the blood-thick sea
   And up from the wreck and rout

And down from the staff on the high cross-tree
Where the flag is signalling out :
    " Keep on."

    The warpath is true and straight,
      It knoweth no left nor right;
    Mars loves not the man who would deviate, —
      For the way to fight is to fight.

            — Chicago Record.

Cuba Libre.

COMES a cry from Cuban water, —
　　From the warm, dusk Antilles, —
From the lost Atlanta's daughter,
　　Drowned in blood as drowned in seas;
Comes a cry of purpled anguish, —
　　See her struggles, hear her cries!
Shall she live, or shall she languish?
　　Shall she sink, or shall she rise?

She shall rise, by all that's holy!
　　She shall live and she shall last;
Rise as we, when crushed and lowly
　　From the blackness of the past.
Bid her strike!　Lo, it is written
　　Blood for blood and life for life.
Bid her smite, as she is smitten;
　　Stars and stripes were born of strife.

Once we flashed her lights of freedom,
　　Lights that dazzled her dark eyes
Till she could but yearning heed them,
　　Reach her hands and try to rise.
Then they stabbed her, choked her, drowned her
　　Till we scarce could hear a note.

Ah! these rusting chains that bound her!
  Oh! these robbers at her throat!

And the kind who forged these fetters?
  Ask five hundred years for news.
Stake and thumbscrew for their betters!
  Inquisitions! Banished Jews!
Chains and slavery! What reminder
  Of one red man in that land?
Why, these very chains that bind her
  Bound Columbus, foot and hand!

She shall rise as rose Columbus,
  From his chains, from shame and wrong, —
Rise as Morning, matchless, wondrous, —
  Rise as some rich morning song, —
Rise a ringing song and story,
  Valor, Love personified.
Stars and stripes espouse her glory,
  Love and Liberty allied.

The Song of Dewey's Guns.

WHAT is this thunder music from the other side
  of the world,
 That pulses through the severing seas and 'round
  the planet runs?
'Tis the death-song of old Spain floating from the
  Asian main;
 There's a tale of crumbling empire in the song of
  Dewey's guns!

The hand that held the sceptre once of all the great
  world seas,
 And paved the march with dead men's bones 'neath
  all the circling suns,
Grew faint with deadly fear when that thunder-song
  drew near,
 For the dirge of Spain was sounded by the song of
  Dewey's guns!

There is music in a cannon yet for all sons of peace, —
 Yea, the port-hole's belching anthem is soft music
  to her sons
When the iron thunder-song sings the death of
  ancient wrong, —
 And a dying wrong was chanted by the song of
  Dewey's guns.

        — *Sam Walter Foss.*

Where Columbia Stands.

COLUMBIA beside the ocean stands,
  And greets the morn with an unclouded brow,
For even now
  Unwonted splendors tinge the conscious sands,
And as she lists,
The world's approval comes from out the mists.

  From the far Orient where beauty dwells,
Where vernal isles wait breathless on her name,
A sweet acclaim
  Comes like the magic whisper of their shells,
And in the cry
She marks the vibrant note of victory!

  With glowing cheek and an enkindled eye,
With confident yet wistful glance she peers,
As now she hears
  The surges where the western Indies lie,
And sees the gleam
Of her ships' wake, fast speeding east, supreme.

  Anon from Cuba comes the hearty hail
Of patriots whose star is beaming bright;

WHERE COLUMBIA STANDS.

After the night
  Of helplessness, crushed by the hand of mail,
Thus left to die,
God hears the dark bondwoman's children cry!

— Arthur Howard Hall.

A Voice from the Old Boys Left Behind.

YES, we marched in the ranks to the station,
　　Escortin' the "boys o' to-day."
An' the youngsters enjoyed the ovation
　　As if 'twas a new kind o' play,
This gift o' young lives to the nation, —
　　A-treadin' on hearts all the day.

The music, the flags, and paradin'
　　Of course lent a mask to our fears;
You'd a-thought we preferred blood to wade in,
　　An' we bid 'em good-by with our cheers.
But somehow our eyesight seemed fadin', —
　　Haven't felt quite so briny for years.

Yes, I know that it's hist'ry repeatin',
　　An' how easy an' natural it came,
When the sixty-one drums were a-beatin'
　　Their rat-tat to glory and fame,
For us to enlist, duty greetin', —
　　But, comrade, this don't seem the same.

We are proud o' the boys, no denyin',
　　But they seemed only boys as they passed
To receive our salute, flags a-flyin',

VOICE FROM THE OLD BOYS LEFT BEHIND.

Too young, and too good to be cast
For our parts in the drama o' dyin',
   Writin' hist'ry in blood hard and fast.

You've noticed the Vets weren't enthusin'
   For the " horrors o' war " to begin,
Till the *Maine* left us small chance for choosin',
   An' humanity's claim led us in.
God knows there's no other excusin'
   This shadow o' hell chasin' sin !

Bein' in, Uncle Sam must keep stayin'
   Till the things settled right, — that's plain;
Meanwhile let the band keep on playin',
   An' the Vets will all join the refrain,
A-mixin' hurrahin' with prayin',
   While the boys do our fightin' with Spain.

God bless 'em, — this new generation, —
   No manlier boys will you find ;
They can whip, man for man, all creation,
   An' we'll have all their glory enshrined
In the hearts o' a united nation, —
   Shake, pard, — tho' they've left us behind !
                    —*John H. Jewett.*

Dewey, Admiral.

K NIGHT of the Eastern seas, thy fadeless fame
      Is writ in War's red blazing letters high
   Upon the backing of that Orient sky,
That glitters with the lustre of thy name;
And tells the Saxon blood doth course the same
      Through all the branches of that mighty tree
      That shades the farthest league of land and sea.
A nation's pride, a race's glad acclaim,
Are thine.   From far Manila's bloody main
We heard the voice of God's new Sinai,
That bade the red requital of thy guns
Wipe out Havana's foul assassin stain.
Avenged at last, our dear dead heroes lie,
An unforgetting land's remembered sons.

— Frank A. Marshall.

To Admiral George Dewey.

YOUNGEST descendant of a glorious line, —
　　Jones, Perry, Hull, Decatur, heroes bold,
　Who fought this nation's brave sea fights of old,
And Farragut, whose great deeds on the brine
Through our wild civil strife with fierce glow
　　　shine, —
　　Dewey, all hail! With theirs is now enrolled
　　Thy name; with theirs thy story will be told;
Thy country's praise and gratitude are thine;
Thy daring sally in Manila Bay
　　Has stirred the whole world's pulse, and well
　　　begun
The war for human rights we wage to-day
　　With consecrated sword.　Hero, well done!
Thy fleet was Heaven-directed in that fray,
　　No grander battle e'er yet fought and won.

　　　　　　　　　　　　—*Virginia Vaughan.*

A Song of the Fleet.

WE'RE faring with the fleet
    Where the ocean billows beat;
Love sends on singing sea-winds his messages so
      sweet;
And speed our brave ships well
Where the ocean thunders swell.
The prayers and tears of Love are theirs, —
    Speed well! Speed well! Speed well!

We're faring with the fleet
Where the isles rejoicing greet
The flag for which the patriot hearts of cheer-
      ing millions beat;
And speed our brave ships well
Till shouts of Victory swell;
The prayers and tears of Love are theirs, —
    Speed well! Speed well! Speed well!

                — *Frank L. Stanton.*

The Awakening of Uncle Sam.

"OH, Uncle Sam," they said, "has grown fat and
    loves his ease,
And he lingers long at table, and distends his
    growing girth ;
The strong arm we used to know has grown slug-
    gard-like and slow,
And they mock his smug indifference to the ends of
    all the earth.

"As his money-bags grow heavy does his love of
    man grow small,
As his cushioned chair grows softer does his cal-
    loused heart grow hard ;
He is careless of his fame, and the glory of his name,
And the vision of the prophet, and the rapture of
    the bard.

"And the tyrants in their anger lash their slaves
    before his eyes,
And he turns his sleepy features tow'rd their faces
    hot with tears,
And he sits between his seas in his soft, voluptuous
    ease,
And the voices of their torment smite his undiscern-
    ing ears."

345

Ah, the slander of the tongues that proclaimed his
    heart was cold!
Ah, the error of the dotage that believed his arm
    was weak!
Ah, the folly, mad and dire, that provoked the slow
    to ire,
And the pride that's in the careless, and the might
    that's in the meek!

He has risen from his feasting, the old look is on his
    face,
For the voices of the helpless and the dying throng
    his path,
For he sees at last their tears, and their groans are in
    his ears,
And his arm is clothed with thunder, and his heart is
    nerved with wrath!

We have wronged him, the forbearing, him the
    patient, slow to smite,
And we love him more than ever, and are prouder of
    his fame;
And we weep the taunts we uttered and whispered
    sneers we muttered, —
For the guns before Manila silenced all the tongues
    of blame.

                    — Sam Walter Foss.

Cuba's Appeal.

O FAIREST of the blue Antilles,
  Scarred by the foeman's sword and steel,
Our hearts leap to thy mute appeal.

Shall we pass with averted eye,
Or but the tribute of a sigh,
Where Cuban brothers, starving, lie?

Where babes wail on the icy breast
Of mothers in their long, last rest,
Dead, amid horrors unexpressed?

Where fathers watch with anguished eye,
While famished children gasp and die,
Their only roof the pitying sky?

Ah, could we deaf and silent be
'Mid all this untold agony,
Nor strike a blow for Cuba free,

Methinks our valiant dead would rise
And, from the depths of sightless eyes,
Transfix us with their mute surprise:

Flashing reproach on you and me,
Heirs of a blood-bought liberty,
That we should live and such things be.

Nay, by the homes we hold so dear,
Never shall rise a wail so drear
And we not hear, and we not hear.

Back to your hills, O men of Spain!
Our war-ships at their anchors strain,
Back! shall the warning sound in vain?

Back to your homes across the waves!
Back to your crosses and your graves!
Plead ye for grace from him who saves!

E'en now too late! what form is this?
Grim in her dread relentlessness,
Within thy gates stands Nemesis!

— Carrie Shaw Rice.

𝔍𝔬𝔦𝔫𝔢𝔡 𝔱𝔥𝔢 𝔅𝔩𝔲𝔢𝔰.

SAYS Stonewall Jackson to " Little Phil: " " Phil,
    have you heard the news ?
Why, our Joe Wheeler — ' Fighting Joe ' — has gone
    and joined the Blues.

" Ay, no mistake, — I saw him come, — I heard the
    oath he took, —
And you'll find it duly entered up in yon great record
    book.

" Yes, Phil, it is a change since then (we give the
    Lord due thanks),
When Joe came sweeping like a hawk upon your
    Sherman's flanks !

" Why, Phil, you knew the trick yourself, — but Joe
    had all the points, —
And we've yet to hear his horses died of stiff or rusty
    joints !

" But what of that? — the deed I saw to-day in
    yonder town
Leads all we did and all Joe did in troopings up and
    down ;

"For, Phil, that oath shall be the heal of many a
    bleeding wound,
And many a Southland song shall yet to that same
    oath be tuned!

"The oath Joe swore has done the work of thrice a
    score of years, —
Ay, more than oath, — he swore away mistrust and
    hate and tears!"

"Yes, yes," says Phil, "he was, indeed, a right good
    worthy foe,
And well he knew, in those fierce days, to give us
    blow for blow!

"When Joe came 'round to pay a call, — the com-
    missaries said, —
Full many a swearing, grumbling 'Yank' went
    supperless to bed;

"He seemed to have a pesky knack — so Sherman
    used to say —
Of calling, when he should by rights be ninety miles
    away!

"Come, Stonewall, put your hand in mine: Joe's
    sworn old Samuel's oath;
We're never North or South again, — he kissed the
    book for both!"

                —*John Lerome Rooney.*

Manila Bay.

THE first great fight of the war is fought !
　And who is the victor, — say, —
Is there aught of the lesson now left untaught
　By the fight of Manila Bay ?

Two by two were the Spanish ships
　Formed in their battle line ;
　　Their flags at the taffrail, peak and fore,
　　And batt'ries ready upon the shore,
　Silently biding their time.

Into their presence sailed our fleet, —
　The harbor was fully mined, —
　　With shotted guns and open ports
　　Up to their ships, — ay, — up to their forts ;
　For Dewey is danger-blind.

Signalled the flagship, " Open fire,"
　And the guns belched forth their death.
　　" At closer range," was the order shown ;
　　Then each ship sprang to claim her own,
　And to lick her fiery breath.

Served were our squadron's heavy guns,
　With gunners stripped to the waist,

And the blinding, swirling, sulph'rous smoke
Enveloped the ships, as each gun spoke,
In its furious, fearful haste.

Sunk and destroyed were the Spanish ships,
Hulled by our heavy shot,
For the Yankee spirit is just the same,
And the Yankee grit and the Yankee aim,
And their courage which faileth not.

The first great fight of the war is fought,
And who is victor, — say, —
Is there aught of the lesson now left untaught
By the fight of Manila Bay?

—*H. E. W., Jr.*

War Prayer.

HELP us to win, O Lord, on sea and land;
  Not by the might alone of armored battle-ships,
    But thy strong hand,
Though all unseen thy shining cohorts must remain;
Help us, for Spain's own sake, to conquer Spain.

Victorious host, which never fought in vain
  On earth's red battle-fields,
Invincible, invisible, nerve the arm
  That Freedom's keen blade wields,
And let the smoke of battle blown away
  By Liberty's free air
With freemen's shouts of victory resound
  Where brave men do and dare.

Strike off Spain's mouldering chains,
  That bind her to a still more mouldering past,
And let her feel the wine of freedom glow
  Through all her veins at last.
Teach her, Columbia, what thyself hast learned
  Through fire and smoke and blood, —
All men are brethren dear alike
  Unto their common father, God.

Teach her that chains of love are stronger far
Than clanking steel or ponderous prison bar;
  Mercy that tempers justice far more meet
  Than despot's lash to bring men to her feet.
Help her, that on her own Castilian shore
The hand of tyranny be felt no more,
And Freedom's banner float from every height
To show that Spain at last has learned
     That right is might.

                    — *M. J. H.*

And Joe Went.

WHEN he heerd the battle-cry
    Joe jes' seemed to set an eye
On to me, much as to say:
"Dad, it's mighty hard to stay!"
Got to mopin' 'round the place
With a battle-hungry face,—
Mopin' like his daddy done
Back in Eighteen Sixty-one.

Once or twice he'd make a break
Liken he was goin' to speak;
Then he'd swaller at a lump
In his throat, an' then the chump
Seemed to weaken, like he thought
His request'd make me hot.
Then he'd sneak away, an' I
Feelin' half inclined to cry.

Grabbed the paper every day
In a sort of nervous way,
An' he'd read the stirrin' news,
Twitchin' to his very shoes.
Bit his lips an' sort o' sighed,
Full o' signs he couldn't hide,

355

Till his mother asked him, " Joe,
What's a-eatin' at you so ? "

" Nothin'," he would say, ' I'm jes'
Nervous like, an' sorter guess
That I'm bilious," then he'd sneak
Over there acrost the creek,
Me a-watchin' him, an' there
I could tell that it was swear
Kep' his lips a-movin' so, —
He was in a stew, was Joe !

Finally I said one day :
" Boy, why don't you say yer say
Like a man, an' not go 'round
Eyes a-draggin' on the ground ?
Long 'fore you were born, yer dad
Had that same, an' had it bad,
An' he went, you bet, — an' Joe,
If you want to go, jes' go ! "

Ort to see him look ! an' — well,
Neighbors said they heerd him yell
Up an' down the creek a mile,
An' you'd ort to seed him pile
On to me an' hug me till
Both my eyes begun to spill,

AND JOE WENT.

An' a lump stuck in my throat
Bigger than a month-old shoat.

   .   .   .   .

Got a letter t'other day
From that Denver camp where they
Are a-rendevooin'.   Joe
Says the cussed rain an' snow
Ain't a bloomin' picnic, yit
He ain't weakenin' a bit,
An' we'll hear from him when he
Goes to set ol' Cuby free.

— Denver Post.

King Coal to Uncle Sam.

I AM the king of strife and calm, —
　　Now a whistle and now a moan, —
I have seized the sceptre and torn the palm
　　From the wind on his bauble throne.
My pipe in his face I boldly puff
　　Till his rage my soul inspires.
And I draw him down and his cries I drown
　　In the glee of a billion fires!
　　　　Oh, I am king of the land and sea,
　　　　　　King of the field and foam,
　　　　King of the mountain, hill, and lea,
　　　　　　King of the hearth and home!

Heir of the lordly limbs and leaves, —
　　Now a whistle and now a moan, —
And my sires, up-garnered in mammoth sheaves,
　　On the floors of the world were strown.
Yet up through the starless roofs I come,
　　And the sentry breezes quail;
And the furnace glow is the flag I throw
　　In the teeth of the howling gale!
　　　　Oh, I am king of the land and sea,
　　　　　　King of the field and foam,

KING COAL TO UNCLE SAM.

King of the mountain, vale, and lea,
  King of the hearth and home!

Tears for the straining sail and sheet, —
  Now a whistle and now a moan, —
As the waves ride over the fated fleet
  At the whim of the wild wind blown.
But cheers for the million-muscled oars
  That I make from drops of rain;
For as coal I am king, and the song I sing
  Is a dirge to the fleet of Spain!
    Oh, I am king of the land and sea,
      King of the field and foam,
    King of the mountain, hill, and lea,
      King of the hearth and home!

                              — *E. F. Burns.*

The Race of the Oregon.

LIGHTS out! And a prow turned towards the
    South,
And a canvas hiding each cannon's mouth,
And a ship like a silent ghost released
Is seeking her sister ships in the East.

A rush of water, a foaming trail,
An ocean hound in a coat of mail,
A deck long-lined with the lines of fate,
She roars good-by at the Golden Gate.

On! On! Alone without gong or bell,
But a burning fire like the fire of hell,
Till the lookout starts as his glasses show
The white cathedral of Callao.

A moment's halt 'neath the slender spire;
Food, food for the men and food for the fire.
Then out to the sea to rest no more
Till her keel is grounded on Chile's shore.

South! South! God guard through the
        unknown wave
Where chart nor compass may help or save,

THE RACE OF THE OREGON.

Where the hissing wraiths of the sea abide
And few may pass through the stormy tide.

North! North! For a harbor far away,
For another breath in the burning day;
For a moment's shelter from speed and pain,
And a prow to the tropic sea again.

Home! Home! With the mother fleet to
     sleep
Till the call shall rise o'er the awful deep;
And the bell shall clang for the battle there,
And the voice of guns is the voice of prayer!

.   .   .   .

One more to the songs of the bold and free,
When your children gather about your knee;
When the Goths and Vandals come down in
     might
As they came to the walls of Rome one night;
When the lordly William of Deloraine
Shall ride by the Scottish lake again;
When the Hessian spectres shall flit in air
As Washington crosses the Delaware;
When the eyes of babes shall be closed in
     dread
As the story of Paul Revere is read:

When your boys shall ask what the guns are
    for,
Then tell them the tale of the Spanish war,
And the breathless millions that looked upon
The matchless race of the *Oregon*.

                —John James Meehan.

Uncover to the Flag.

UNCOVER to the flag; bare head
  Sorts well with heart as, humbly
    bowed,
We stand in presence of the dead
  Who make the flag their shroud.

Uncover to the flag, for there
  The patriot past is typified,
Of those who taught us how to dare
  For liberty, and died.

Uncover to the flag, for those
  Of Concord and of Bunker Hill,
The first to fire on freedom's foes,
  With shots that echo still.

Uncover to the flag, for him
  Who sang the song, the gallant Key,
When in the dawn hour, gray and dim,
  He strained, its stars to see.

Uncover to the flag, for one
  Who scorned to have his colors dip,
And fighting all but flying none,
  Cried, " Don't give up the ship."

Uncover to the flag, for him
  Who stoutly nailed it to the mast,
And dauntlessly, or sink or swim,
  Stood by it to the last.

Uncover to the flag; the land
  It floats above is one anew, —
The North and South, now hand in hand,
  See God's skies, gray and blue.

Uncover to the flag; it flew
  Above the men who manned the *Maine*,
The pledge that we will mete the due
  Of vengeance out to Spain!

Uncover to the flag; it stands
  For all of bravest, all of best,
In us with flower-laden hands,
  In those who lie at rest.
            — *E. C. Cheverton.*

Enlisted.

The Old Soldier Speaks.

I FOUGHT under Lee and Stonewall,
　And I hated a Yankee like sin,
But gimme my uniform, sergeant,
　I'm going to fight ag'in.

I took out my old gray clothes last night,
　I thought of the day they was new,
And I looked at the holes in the left-hand
　　　sleeve
Where a minie ball went through.

And I heard the band play " Dixie," —
　By God! I heard every note, —
And I thought of Manassas and Shiloh,
　And a lump came up in my throat.

And I said, " Go back to that old oak chest,
　There ain't no more service for you;
I'm goin' to fight on the side that's right,
　And I'm going to wear the blue!"

There's jest one thought in every heart,
　One word in every mouth;

For things is all so twisted around
   That there ain't no North nor South.

I never thought it would come to this;
   It's strange, but I reckon it's true;
For it's jest one country and jest one flag,
   And we're all a-wearin' the blue !

            — Eliza Calvert Hall.

The Men Behind the Guns.

A CHEER and salute for the admiral, and here's to
the captain bold,
And never forget the commodore's debt when the
deeds of might are told!
They stand to the deck thro' the battle's wreck, when
the great shells roar and screech, —
And never they fear when the foe is near to practise
what they preach;
But off with your hat and three times three for
Columbia's true-blue sons, —
The men below who batter the foe, — the men behind
the guns!

Oh, light and merry of heart are they when they
swing into port once more,
When, with more than enough of the "green-backed
stuff," they start for their leave-o'-shore;
And you'd think, perhaps, that the blue-bloused chaps
who loll along the street
Are a tender bit, with salt on it, for some "mustache"
to eat, —

Some warrior bold, with straps of gold, who dazzles
    and fairly stuns
The modest worth of the sailor boys, — the lads who
    serve the guns.

But say not a word till a shot is heard that tells the
    fight is on,
Till the long deep roar grows more and more from
    the ships of " Yank " and " Don,"
Till over the deep the tempests sweep of fire and
    bursting shell,
And the very air is a mad Despair in the throes of a
    living hell;
Then down, deep down, in the mighty ship, unseen by
    the midday suns,
You'll find the chaps who are giving the raps, — the
    men behind the guns !

Oh, well they know how the cyclones blow that they
    loose from their cloud of wrath,
And they know is heard the thunder-word their fierce
    ten-inchers saith !
The steel decks rock with the lightning shock, and
    shake with the great recoil,
And the sea grows red with the blood of the dead and
    reaches for its spoil, —

THE MEN BEHIND THE GUNS.

But not till the foe has gone below, or turns his prow
    and runs,
Shall the voice of peace bring sweet release to the
    men behind the guns !

—John James Rooney.

Dewey in Manila Bay.

HE took a thousand islands and he didn't lose a
    man —
  (Raise your heads and cheer him as he goes!)
He licked the sneaky Spaniard till the fellow cut and
    ran,
  For fighting's part of what a Yankee knows.

He fought 'em and he licked 'em, and he didn't give
    a d——
  (It was only his profession for to win),
He sank their boats beneath 'em, and he spared 'em
    as they swam,
  And then he sent his ambulances in.

He had no word to cheer him and had no bands to
    play,
  He had no crowds to make his duty brave;
But he risked the deep torpedoes at the breaking of
    the day,
  For he knew he had our self-respect to save.

He flew the angry signal crying justice for the *Maine,*
  He flew it from his flagship as he fought.
He drove the tardy vengeance in the very teeth of
    Spain,
  And he did it just because he thought he ought.

DEWEY IN MANILA BAY.

He busted up their batteries, and sank eleven ships
   (He knew what he was doing, every bit);
He set the Maxims going like a hundred cracking
     whips,
   And every shot that crackled was a hit.

He broke 'em and he drove 'em, and he didn't care
     at all,
   He only liked to do as he was bid;
He crumpled up their squadron and their batteries
     and all, —
   He knew he had to lick 'em, and he did.

And when the thing was finished and they flew the
     frightened flag,
   He slung his guns and sent his foot ashore,
And he gathered in their wounded, and he quite
     forgot to brag,
   For he thought he did his duty, nothing more.

Oh, he took a thousand islands and he didn't lose a
     man —
   (Raise your heads and cheer him as he goes!)
He licked the sneaky Spaniard till the fellow cut and
     ran,
   For fighting's part of what a Yankee knows!
               — *R. V. Risley.*

The Spirit of the Maine.

I N battle-line of sombre gray
  Our ships of war advance,
As Red Cross knights in holy fray
  Charged with avenging lance.
And terrible shall be thy plight,
  O fleet of cruel Spain!
For ever in our van doth fight
  The spirit of the *Maine !*

As when, beside Regillus Lake,
  The great twin brethren came
A righteous fight for Rome to make
  Against a deed of shame,
So now a ghostly ship shall doom
  The fleet of treacherous Spain, —
Before her guilty soul doth loom
  The spirit of the *Maine !*

A wraith arrayed in peaceful white,
  As when asleep she lay
Above the traitorous mine that night
  Within Havana Bay,

THE SPIRIT OF THE MAINE.

She glides before the avenging fleet
  A sign of woe to Spain.
Brave though her sons, how shall they
       meet
  The spirit of the *Maine?*

                 — *Tudor Jenks.*

The New Memorial Day.

" Under the roses the blue;
Under the lilies the gray."

OH, the roses we plucked for the
blue,
And the lilies we twined for the gray,
We have bound in a wreath,
And in silence beneath
Slumber our heroes to-day.

Over the new-turned sod
The sons of our fathers stand,
And the fierce old fight
Slips out of sight
In the clasp of a brother's hand.

For the old blood left a stain
That the new has washed away,
And the sons of those
That have faced as foes
Are marching together to-day.

Oh, the blood that our fathers gave!
Oh, the tide of our mothers' tears!

THE NEW MEMORIAL DAY.

And the flow of red,
And the tears they shed,
   Embittered a sea of years.

But the roses we plucked for the
      blue,
  And the lilies we twined for the
      gray
We have bound in a wreath,
And in glory beneath
  Slumber our heroes to-day !

          —Albert Bigelow Paine.

Spain's Hour of Doom.

Written on the declaration of Cuban independence
by the American Congress.

SPAIN'S hour has struck.   No more her
flag
Shall float o'er Cuba's fateful isle.
Her reign of treachery and guile
Is o'er.   No more shall vengeance lag.

Back to their gaunt Iberian crag
Her desolating legions hurl,
Or let the wild Atlantic's swirl
Their souls and bodies hellward drag.

Ay, let her new armada flee
Westward her tyranny to maintain.
We will, in memory of the *Maine*,
Meet it and sink it in the sea.

Out of the Western Hemisphere
Spain's yellow banner soon shall fade.
No more by her shall graves be made
Where grain should grow and fruits appear.

SPAIN'S HOUR OF DOOM.

No more her fiends with sword and fire
   The Cubans' homes shall devastate,
   Slay sons, and daughters violate
Before their mother and their sire.

The infamy of Spain shall loom
   Black over the devoted isle
   No longer.   Not by force or will
Can she put back the hour of doom.

That hour has struck.   From Morro's height
   Haul down her old dishonored flag,
   While back to her Iberian crag,
She takes her ignominious flight.

                —Albert Roland Haven.

Dewey at Manila.

'TWAS the very verge of May
    When the bold *Olympia* led
Into Bocagrande Bay
    Dewey's squadron, dark and dread, —
Creeping past Corregidor,
Guardian of Manila's shore.

Do they sleep who wait the fray?
    Is the moon so dazzling bright
That our cruisers' battle-gray
    Melts into the misty light?
Ah! the red flash and the roar!
Wakes at last Corregidor!

All too late her screaming shell
    Tears the silence with its track;
This is but the *gate* to hell,
    We've no leisure to turn back.
Answer, *Concord!* — then once more
Slumber on, Corregidor.

And as, like a slowing tide,
    Onward still the vessels creep,
Dewey, watching, falcon-eyed,

DEWEY AT MANILA.

Orders, — "Let the gunners sleep;
For we meet a foe at four
Fiercer than Corregidor."

Well they slept, for well they knew
　What the morrow taught us all, —
He was wise (as well as true)
　Thus upon the foe to fall.
Long shall Spain the day deplore
Dewey ran Corregidor.

May is dancing into light
　As the Spanish admiral
From a dream of phantom fight
　Wakens at his sentry's call.
Shall he leave Cavite's lee,
Hunt the Yankee fleet at sea?

O Montojo, to thy deck,
　That to-day shall float its last!
Quick! To quarters! Yonder speck
　Grows a hull of portent vast.
Hither, toward Cavite's lee
Comes the Yankee hunting thee!

Not for fear of hidden mine
　Halts our quiet commodore.
He, of old heroic line,

Follows Farragut once more,
Hazards all on victory,
Here within Cavite's lee.

If he loses, all is gone ;
 He will win because he must.
And the shafts of yonder dawn
 Are not quicker than his thrust.
Soon, Montojo, he shall be
With thee in Cavite's lee.

Now, Manila, to the fray !
 Show the hated Yankee host
This is not a holiday, —
 Spanish blood is more than boast.
Fleet and mine and battery,
Crush him in Cavite's lee !

Lo, hell's geysers at our fore
 Pierce the plotted path, — in vain,
Nerving every man the more
 With the memory of the *Maine !*
Now at last our guns are free
Here within Cavite's lee.

" Gridley," says the commodore,
 " You may fire when ready." Then
Long and loud, like lions' roar

DEWEY AT MANILA.

When a rival dares the den,
Breaks the awful cannonry
Full across Cavite's lee.

Who shall tell the daring tale
   Of our Thunderbolt's attack,
Finding, when the chart should fail,
   By the lead his dubious track,
Five ships following faithfully
Five times o'er Cavite's lee ;

Of our gunners' deadly aim ;
   Of the gallant foe and brave
Who, unconquered, faced with flame,
   Seek the mercy of the wave, —
Choosing honor in the sea
Underneath Cavite's lee ?

Let the meed the victors gain
   Be the measure of their task.
Less of flinching, stouter strain,
   Fiercer combat, who could ask ?
And "surrender," — 'twas a word
That Cavite never heard.

Noon, — the woful work is done !
   Not a Spanish ship remains;
But, of their eleven, none

381

Ever was so truly Spain's!
Which is prouder, they or we,
Thinking of Cavite's lee?

ENVOY.

But remember, when we've ceased
  Giving praise and reckoning odds,
Man shares courage with the beast,
  Wisdom cometh from the gods.
Who would win, on land or wave,
Must be wise as well as brave.

— Robert Underwood Johnson.

1898 and 1562.

THE evening and the morning have joined in fight
    at last.
  Around the Western islands the Old shall fight the
    New;
Columbia and Hispania, the Present and the Past,
  And Eighteen Hundred and Ninety-eight fights
    Fifteen Sixty-two.

The Nation of the Forward Look that sees the
    heights ahead
  Fights with the Backward Glancing Realm that
    sees the tombs behind.
And who shall doubt the conflict of the Quick and of
    the Dead, —
  Of the Leaders with the Laggards of Mankind?

To-day joins fight with Yesterday; the mediæval
    years
  Are grappling with the Modern, and the Old
    assails the New.
But who, who fears the issue? Where's the trem-
    bling soul that fears
  When Eighteen Hundred Ninety-eight fights Fif-
    teen Sixty-two?

— Sam Walter Foss.

An American to His Mother.

DOST thou hear, Columbia, O my mother,
  That pale suppliant, sobbing at thy feet, —
Spat upon, and stripped, and left to starve there,
  Naked in the street ?

With her feeble strength she gropes to grasp thee, —
  But to touch thy hem, and rise up free.
Listen ! Shall her blue lips, drawn with hunger,
  Call in vain on thee ?

Oh, her white and branded beauty, mother !
  Oh, her virgin, violated fame !
Crawling to thy knees, she cries in anguish,
  " Save me from this shame !

" By thy sons that hung against thy bosom,
  Sucking from thy veins their stalwart breath ;
By the blood they spilt to guard thy honor, —
  Save me from this death !

" By thy daughters' fame, thine own fair virtue ;
  By thy motherhood, that all men know ;
By the unborn Future in thy loins, —
  Kill this loathsome foe ! "

AN AMERICAN TO HIS MOTHER.

Wouldst thou harken, lend thine eyes, stretch hands
     of succor?
  Useless!   Unless, first, thy vengeance rain
In a leaden storm on her seducer.
  Strike!— God pity Spain!

— Boston Journal.

His New Suit.

I REMEMBER well the way
    She looked up at me that day
When I first put on the gray,
    And said good-by, back there in '63.
She and I were sweethearts then,
And I hear her voice again,
    As she nestled up to me,
Saying, in her gentle way:
" Ah, how brave you look in gray,
And how tall and handsome, too, —
Gray's the color, dear, for you ! "

There's a ragged suit of gray
She has long had laid away, —
    There are memories that cling around
        it, too ;
But the years have come and gone,
And at present I have on
    A suit of Uncle Sam's beloved blue.

When she saw me yesterday,
She wiped a tear away
For the memory of the gray, —
    That dear, old, ragged suit of '63.

And she sweetly spoke again, —
Spoke more fervently than then, —
   As she nestled up to me,
Saying, in her gentle way:
" Ah, how brave you looked in gray !
But you're braver still in blue, —
Blue's the color, dear, for you ! "

                   —*S. E. Kiser.*

To the Flying Squadron.

FIERCE flock of sea gulls, with huge wings of
    white,
    Tossed on the treacherous blue,
Poising your pinions in majestic flight, —
    Our hearts take voyage with you.

Against the soulless, unregarding Sea
    Match the high will that dares !
Are ye not driven by mightier gales than she ? —
    Millions of patriot prayers !

Flock of the terrible talons ! — urged by lungs
    Monstrous and fury-fed !
Hold your proud course till rot their riotous tongues, ·
    Fear-born and treason-bred,

Who at this late and ominous hour declaim
    The jargon of the past, —
Forgetful fools, that Freedom, that great name,
    Hath riven all chains at last.

God save us from war's terrors !   May they cease !
    And yet one fate how worse !
A bloodless, perjured, prostituting peace,
    Glutting a coward's purse !

TO THE FLYING SQUADRON.

Oh, if yon beaks and talons clutch and cling
    Far in the middle seas
With those of hostile war birds, wing to wing, —
    Our hearts shall fight with these.

God speed you!   Never fared crusading knight
    On holier quest than ye, —
Sworn to the rescue of the trampled Right, —
    Sworn to make Cuba free! —

Yea, swiftly to avenge our martyred *Maine*.
    I watch you curve and wheel
In horrible grace of battle, — scourge of Spain,
    Birds with the beaks of steel!

The Recompense.

THEY are marching from the Southland, from the
North, and from the West,
From the sunny hills of vintage, from the crags
where eagles nest,
From the altars of devotion, from a mother's loving
breast,
While above them floats Old Glory, boon to all the
world oppressed.

They are marching to the ocean where the crimsoned
waters cry,
Where the cowards jeered in anger, laughed to see
our heroes die,
Little dreaming that in vengeance God was watching
from on high,
That he heard the blood-stained billows lift their
voices to the sky.

There's a song comes from the forest, there's a song
breaks from the sea,
And the echoes ring from heaven in tumultuous
ecstasy ;
For the flag floats high in splendor, our old flag of
liberty,

THE RECOMPENSE.

Where the mists of night are lifting, and God's
    people are made free.

Oh, be brave, my heart, with courage, and my soul,
    be ever strong!
To the right or left turn never, but press fearlessly
    along;
For the God above hath vengeance, and shall recom-
    pense the wrong,
Till the wrath of man shall praise him, and the
    darkness break with song!

                          — Chas. H. Dorrie.

Reunited.

I 'VE been thinkin' of it over, an' it 'pears to me
    to-day
The war's the biggest blessin' that has ever come
    our way;
Course, thar'll be some fightin', an' a few more
    graves'll be
Whar the daisies in the medder look their purtiest
    at me, —

For that's to be expected; but — the thing that
    makes me feel
That the war's a heavenly blessin' is the wounds that
    it'll heal!
The old wounds that's been ranklin' sence the day
    that Gin'rul Lee
Said we'd rest an' think it over by that old-time
    apple-tree!

I see the boys that fit us in the Union coats of blue
On the same groun', — hale an' hearty, an' a-shakin'
    howdy-do!
An' I hear the ban' play "Dixie," an' I see 'em
    march away,
Till I can't tell whar the blue is, an' I'm mixed up
    on the gray!

REUNITED.

The old war tunes air ringin', an' "Dixie's" on the
    rise;
But "Yankee Doodle" follers 'fore it's half-way to
    the skies!
An' the old "Star Spangled Banner" is in ever'
    steeple's chime,
An' I tell you, we're a-havin' of a hallelujah time!

I'm glad I've lived to see it; I'm glad the time is
    come
When, North an' South, we answer to the roll-call of
    the drum!
When thar ain't no line divides us, but North an'
    South we stan'
For jest one common country, — one freedom-lovin'
    lan'!

That's whar the war's a blessin', that's whar 'pears
    like I see
A brighter mornin' breakin' on the hills for you
    an' me!
It's shoulder now to shoulder, — thar ain't no blue or
    gray, —
An' we're shoutin' "Hallelujah," an' we're happy on
    the way!

                        — *F. L. Stanton.*

"Cut the Cables."

An Incident of Cienfuegos.

" CUT the cables ! " the order read,
　　And the men were there ; there was no delay.
The ships hove to in Cienfuegos Bay, —
　　The *Windom, Nashville, Marblehead*, —
Beautiful, grim, and alert were they,
It was midway, past in the morning gray.
　　" Cut the cables ! " the order said —
Over the clouds of the dashing spray
The guns were trained and ready for play ;
　　Picked from the *Nashville*, Winslow led, —
Grim death waits ashore, they say ;
" Lower the boats, Godspeed, give way."
Did " our untried navy lads " obey ?
　　Away to their perilous work they sped.

Now, steady the keel, keep stroke the oar !
　　They must go in close, they must find the wires ;
Grim death is alert on that watching shore,
　　That deadly shore of the " Hundred Fires."
In the lighthouse tower, — along the ledge, —
　　In the blockhouse, waiting, — the guns are there ;
On the lowland, too, in the tall, dry sedge ;

"CUT THE CABLES."

They are holding the word till the boats draw
    near.
One hundred feet from the water's edge,
    Dazzling clear is the sunlit air;
Quick, my men, — the moments are dear!
    Two hundred feet from the rifle-pit,
And our " untried " lads still show no fear —
    When they open now they're sure to hit;
No question, even by sign, they ask,
In silence they bend to their dangerous task.

Quick now! — the shot from a smokeless gun
    Cuts close and spatters the glistening brine;
Now follows the roar of the battle begun,
But the boys were bent in the blazing sun
    Like peaceful fishermen, " wetting a line."
They searched the sea while a shrieking blast
    Swept shoreward, swift as the lightning flies, —
While the fan-like storm of the shells went past
    Like a death-wing cleaving the hissing skies.
Like a sheltering wing, — for the hurricane came
    From our own good guns, and the foe might tell
What wreck was wrought by their deadly aim;
    For the foe went down where the hurricane fell.
It shattered the blockhouse, levelled the tower,
    It ripped the face of the smoking hill,
It beat the battle back, hour by hour,

And then, for a little, our guns were still.
For a little, but that was the fatal breath, —
That moment's lull in the friendly crash, —
For the long pit blazed with a vicious flash,
And eight fell, — two of them done to death.

Once more the screen of the screaming shot
With its driving canopy covered the men,
While they dragged, and grappled, and, faltering not,
Still dragged, and searched, and grappled again.
And they stayed right there till the work was done,
The cables were found and severed, each one,
With an eighty-foot gap, and the " piece " hauled in,
And stowed in place, — then, under the din
Of that deafening storm, that had swept the air
For three long hours, they turned from shore
(" Steady the keel " there; " stroke " the oar),
To the smoke-wreathed ships, and, under the guns,
They went up the side, — our " untried " ones.

Quiet, my brave boys; hats off, all!
They are here, our " untried " boys in blue.
Steady the block, now, all hands haul!
Slow on the line there! — look to that crew!
Six lads hurt! — and the colors there?
Wrap two of them ? — hold! Ease back the bow!
Slow, now, on the line ! — slack down with care!

"CUT THE CABLES."

Steady! — they're back on their own deck now!
The cables are cut, sir, eighty-foot spread,
Six boys hurt, and — two of them dead.
　　Half-mast the colors! there's work to do!
There are two red marks on the starboard gun,
There is still some work that is not quite done,
　　For our "untried" boys that are tried and true.
It wasn't all play when they cut the wires, —
Well named is that bay of the "Hundred Fires."

　　　　　　　　　— *Robert Burns Wilson.*

June 2, 1898.

"Mene, Mene, Tekel, Upharsin."

BEHOLD, we have gathered together our battle-
　　ships, near and afar;
Their decks they are cleared for action, their guns
　　they are primed for war.
From the East to the West there is hurry; in the
　　North and the South a peal
Of hammers in fort and shipyard, and the clamor
　　and clang of steel;
And the rush and roar of engines, and clanking of
　　derrick and crane, —
Thou art weighed in the scales and found wanting,
　　the balance of God, O Spain!

Behold, I have stood on the mountains, and this was
　　writ in the sky:
" She is weighed in the scales and found wanting, the
　　balance God holds on high !"
The balance he once weighed Babylon, the Mother of
　　Harlots, in.
One scale holds thy pride and power and empire, be-
　　gotten of sin,
Heavy with woe and torture, the crimes of a thou-
　　sand years,

Mortared and welded together with fire and blood
    and tears ;
In the other, for justice and mercy, a blade with
    never a stain,
Is laid the Sword of Liberty, and the balance dips,
    O Spain !

Summon thy vessels together ! great is thy need for
    these !
Cristobal Colon, Vizcaya, Oquendo, and *Marie The-*
rese.
Let them be strong and many, for a vision I had by
    night,
That the ancient wrongs thou hast done the world
    came howling to the fight;
From the New World shores they gathered. Inca and
    Aztec, slain,
To the Cuban shot but yesterday, and our own dead
    seamen, Spain !

Summon thy ships together, gather a mighty fleet !
For a strong young nation is arming that never hath
    known defeat.
Summon thy ships together, there on thy blood-
    stained sands !
For a shadowy army gathers with manacled feet and
    hands,

399

A shadowy host of sorrows and of shames, too black
 to tell,
That reach with their horrible wounds for thee to
 drag thee down to hell;
Myriad phantoms and spectres, thou warrest against
 in vain!
Thou art weighed in the scales and found wanting,
 the balance of God, O Spain!

     — Madison Cawein.

Fall In!

'TIS no time for vain surmising;
      Fall in!
While the din of war is rising;
      Fall in!
See the cloud of conflict falling,
Though the danger is appalling;
Hark! your country's voice is calling:
      Fall in!

Past, the time for speculation;
      Fall in!
Peril menaces the nation;
      Fall in!
Leave to cravens idle prattle;
Empty vessels loudest rattle!
Trusting in the God of battle;
      Fall in!

Waste no precious time in trifles;
      Fall in!
Drop all else and grasp your rifles;
      Fall in!
Lay your lives on country's altar,
Cursed the craven who would falter,
For the traitor's neck the halter!
      Fall in!

Son and sire and grandsire hoary,
Fall in !
Insult stains our grand " Old Glory ! "
Fall in !
By our tars 'neath ocean sleeping,
Billowy mounds above them heaping,
By the tears their loved are weeping,
Fall in !

Spirit of the Revolution !
Fall in !
Reinforce our resolution ;
Fall in !
North and South now reunited,
Union's covenant replighted,
Fire on Freedom's shrine relighted !
Fall in !

—Frank N. Scott.

The Old Artillerist.

H E never has talked of the war-time and battle,
  He gives himself wholly to peace and its ways
And he loves his small fields and his horses and
    cattle,
  And the smell of the corn fields through long sum-
    mer days.
It seems like a dream in his calm daily labors,
  That once he fought fiercely where swift bullets
    smote,
But always on Sundays at church with his neighbors
  A little bronze button is worn on his coat.

The sixties had found him where bugles rang charges,
  Where over the batteries the cavalry rode,
And the smoke of the guns hung along the field's
    marges
  As hotly the battle's tide eddying flowed.
His boy's heart had thrilled at the reverberation,
  As, plying the sponge or the lanyard, he toiled;
His smoke-stifled throat throbbed with fierce exultation
  The while he stood by till the piece had recoiled.

But now!—not a word of the war-time and battle,
  No tales of the conflict the veteran will tell;

He's at peace in his fields with his horses and cattle,
   Who once had been rained on by bullet and shell.
But he chuckles, these days, as he plods at his labors,
   Because his two boys have enlisted, and he
Walks straighter and prouder when passing the
     neighbors,
   For Bill is with Dewey and Jim is with Lee!
                — *Meredith Nicholson.*

Greeting from England.

AMERICA! dear brother land!
   While yet the shotted guns are mute,
   Accept a brotherly salute,
A hearty grip of England's hand.

To-morrow, when the sulphurous glow
   Of war shall dim the stars above,
   Be sure the star of England's love
Is over you, come weal or woe.

Go forth in hope!   Go forth in might!
   To all your nobler self be true,
   That coming times may see in you
The vanguard of the hosts of light.

Though wrathful justice load and train
   Your guns, be every breach they make
   A gateway pierced for mercy's sake
That peace may enter in and reign.

Then, should the hosts of darkness band
   Against you, lowering thunderously,
   Flash the word " Brother " o'er the sea,
And England at your side shall stand,

Exulting!   For, though dark the night
  And sinister with scud and rack,
  The hour that brings us back to back
But harbingers the larger light.

April 22, 1898.   *— London Chronicle.*

𝕳𝖔𝖇𝖘𝖔𝖓 𝖆𝖓𝖉 𝕳𝖎𝖘 𝕸𝖊𝖓.

O N the girdling circuit,
　　Under sundered seas,
Over dale and mountain,
　　Caught by ev'ry breeze,
Glory sends a message
　　(Cipherless her pen)
That the world is cheering
　　Hobson and his men!

CHORUS.

Eight against the fleet and forts, —
　　A brook against a sea!
But Santiago's door is shut
　　And Hobson turned the key!

Moon behind a cloud-bank,
　　Fickle Cuban sky,
Hobson and his seven tars
　　Steaming boldly by!
Phillips, Murphy, Deignan,
　　Clausen and Charette,
Montagu and Kelly,
　　Not a man forget! — Cho.

407

Right athwart the channel, —
   Hobson's heart the guide, —
Swung the bulky collier
   Hinged upon the tide.
Growled the guns of Spaniards,
   Growled from either shore ;
But, his sea legs keeping,
   Hobson hung his door ! — Cho.

Soon shall legions thunder,
   Cannoned mountains rock,
And that door swing open
   Wide at Freedom's knock !
High at Santiago
   Rear a column then,
Bidding Time remember
   Hobson and his men ! — Cho.

                — *Edward F. Burns.*

Prayer for the Nation.

JUDGE of the earth, to whom
  The secret things are known,
Lo, in this hour of gloom,
  We come before thy throne.
The knees of Freedom's sons are bent
  To none, O Lord, but thee;
Before thy altar we present
  Our motive and our plea.

Thou knowest all the cause, —
  The crime and insult both, —
Long have we taken pause,
  And even now are loth
To strike the blow, — yet Honor calls,
  Her summons we obey;
Fit mate were he for knaves and thralls
  Who yet would urge delay.

Not for ourselves we try
  The final test of war, —
A tortured people cry
  For succor from afar;
Before the bar of Liberty
  Stands Tyranny arraigned:

The cup she mixed of misery
Shall by herself be drained.

If with a hand unclean
We wrongly draw the sword,
We pray thee intervene
To make our cause abhorred.
We would not dim a history
In honor clear begun.
We crave, O Lord, no victory
That is not justly won.

Let other nations sneer;
Accountable alone
To thee, O Lord, we fear
No censure save thine own.
The Powers of earth are in thy sight
A pageant and a dream;
Thou ever art of Truth and Right
The arbiter supreme.

The trumpet calls us forth;
The fateful guns are trained;
Oh, may we prove our worth,
Our honor keep unstained!

PRAYER FOR THE NATION.

We lift the gage; the issue stands
   For innocence or guilt;
Our cause we place within thy hands, —
   Deal with us as thou wilt.

             — *Boston Transcript.*

The Sailing of the Fleet.

TWO fleets have sailed from Spain. The one
would seek
What lands uncharted ocean might conceal.
Despised, condemned, and pitifully weak,
It found a world for Leon and Castile.

The other, mighty, arrogant, and vain,
Sought to subdue a people who were free.
Ask of the storm-gods where its galleons be, —
Whelmed 'neath the billows of the northern main!

A third is threatened. On the westward track,
Once gloriously traced, its vessels speed,
With gold and crimson battle-flags unfurled.
On Colon's course, but to Sidonia's wrack,
Sure fated, if so need shall come to need,
For sons of Drake are lords of Colon's world.

— *The New York Tribune.*

Eight Volunteers.

EIGHT volunteers! on an errand of death!
  Eight men! Who speaks?
Eight men to go where the cannon's hot breath
  Burns black the cheeks.
Eight men to man the old *Merrimac's* hulk;
Eight men to sink the old steamer's black bulk,
Blockade the channel where Spanish ships skulk, —
  Eight men! Who speaks?

" Eight volunteers! " said the Admiral's flags!
  Eight men! Who speaks?
Who will sail under El Morro's black crags? —
  Sure death he seeks.
Who is there willing to offer his life?
Willing to march to this music of strife, —
Cannon for drum and torpedo for fife?
  Eight men! Who speaks?

Eight volunteers! on an errand of death!
  Eight men! Who speaks?
Was there a man who in fear held his breath?
  With fear-paled cheeks?

From ev'ry war-ship ascended a cheer!
From ev'ry sailor's lips burst the word "Here!"
Four thousand heroes their lives volunteer!
  Eight men!   Who speaks?
                              — *Lansing C. Bailey.*

FLING OUT THE FLAG.

BY THOMAS NIELD.

Fling out the flag in freedom's name and let it flutter
    free,
A terror to the tyrant dons who came across the sea—
The European centipedes that poison where they tread,
And leave in every land they touch a ghastly heap of
    dead.
Remember Torquemada's rack and Alva's houndish
    crew,
How Cortez harried Mexico, Pizarro cursed Peru,
An Weyler wrote on Cuban soil the Spaniard's bloody
    name;
Then float, O flag, in triumph o'er the graveyard of their
    shame.

Fling out the flag in victory's name, which brightens all
    its stars,
And gives a rainbow splendor to the rose hue of its bars.
Wide let it flap o'er sunken ships and battle battered
    walls,
Until the last hope of the dons before its presence falls.
Remind them of Manila and of Santiago's fate;
As hints of retribution that may yet their crimes await;
Aye, make them tremble as they hear our nearing can-
    nons roar,
Until they take their poisonous feet from every foreign
    shore.

Fling out the flag in glory's name, but let that glory be
To drive the tyrant to his den and set his victims free;
Then let the eagle roar and scream o'er freedom's lofty
    crags,
While in the valley's dust we drag the foe's dishonored
    rags.
Convince the sordid nations that we have both will and
    power
To act the good Samaritan in dark oppression's hour.
Display the true ideal of the duty of the strong
To save a weaker neighbor from the talons of the wrong.

Fling out the flag in heaven's high name, that heaven
    may bless anew
That sacred emblem of the right with blessings like the
    dew;
And while it flutters let us trust in Him to guard our
    land
Who holds the fate of nations in the hollow of his hand.
Remember him in sunshine who remembered us in shade,
For in the present triumph is the former power displayed;
And in the march of progress let us ever keep the van,
And lead the nations on to own the brotherhood of man.

www.ingramcontent.com/pod-product-compliance
Lightning Source LLC
Chambersburg PA
CBHW030956110726
47900CB00004B/1299